DARKER

THE MAW OF MAYHEM MC
BOOK 2

AK NEVERMORE

TABLE OF CONTENTS

FREE PREQUEL

CATS DON'T ALWAYS *LAND ON THEIR FEET...*

Grimdarke James has got problems. As Vice Prez of the Maw of Mayhem MC, he needs to keep his shit together, but between the constant threat of his inner cat going feral, and Nikki, one of the motorcycle club's mollys, blackmailing him, it's a fine line some days.

Then when an arms deal goes bad, everything goes to hell with it. All fingers point to an old club enemy, a man Grim has reason to both fear and loathe, but the facts don't add up, and everyone is a suspect... including Grim. Faced with the constant threat of Nikki revealing his past and his need to prove himself to the MC, the fragile peace he's made with his cat is threatened.

Out of options and running out of time, Grim sets a bold

plan into motion, and the consequences are far more dire than he could have imagined…

Download it at: bit.ly/readmayhem

AND FOR MORE SHORT stories from the world of the Maw of Mayhem MC, check out:

bit.ly/bitesofmayhem

DEDICATION

This one is for Mags, who, when asked if it was too dirty, said, "Wait, is that even a thing?"

CONTENT WARNING

Heads up & don't try this at home: This book explores themes which some readers may find uncomfortable or offensive. If violence, smut, various kinks, salty language, drug use, casting shade at pickles, and generally unsavory behavior are triggers for you, please put this novella down and back away slowly.

BEFORE

SHADES of the past tore through the consciousness Darke shared with his man, threatening to swallow Grim whole. He fought against their poisoned bite, but the witch's spell had weakened the big cat's skin-brother and freed the memories from their fetters. They lashed at Grim with inky black tentacles of torment. His agonized screams rose within the crescendoing squall, raging through their split psyche. A growl welled in Darke's chest, ruff bristling at their assault.

—*Mine!*— he snarled, lunging into the fray. Sharp claws and teeth rent the shadowed memories of the bad time from his man, scattering them back into the depths of their mind. Grim was his. Him. A self separate, yet one. His skin-brother. Darke nuzzled him close, tongue rasping over Grim's flickering light.

—*heal*—

Kit... his man whimpered, curling into a ball. His light dimmed, giving up control of their form to the big cat.

—*ours*— Darke rumbled, shifting their body and sending Grim what strength he could. Fur sprouted, limbs cracking and reforming. Two legs became four, and a tawny gray mountain lion lay sprawled on the bed where the others had lain his man to recover.

Within, his skin-brother's light strengthened, its low glow holding steady.

Darke ran a paw over his face, licking at his pad. He sneezed at the scent of old blood, the room thick with the patina of its tang and the decaying musk of the undead. A low growl rumbled in his chest, his pupils dilating to take in the room's blend of muted color.

Heavy furniture dominated the space, its angles stark amidst the gloom. Tendrils of scent threaded through the room, age and linseed seeping from the wood to twine with the rest of the civilized rot assaulting his nose. He pushed off the bed, padding across the thick carpet. His shadow grayed the fingers of scant moonlight streaming in from long, amber-tinted windows.

Darke paused, his lip curling over his canines, disdainfully eyeing the city spread out below him before turning his face to the bulbous moon.

Had Grim's female changed and released her animal?

Clay's cat had promised Darke a mate. Teased him with her scent, captured within the weft of the afghan on Grim's bed. The desperate longing it evoked proved the connection. The tip of Darke's tail twitched. He'd trusted it would be so. Waited for so long. Too long. Kit's scent matched the afghan's. That meant the beast within her was his.

Darke chuffed his frustration. Sensing his mate without being able to claim her was torture. He paced the breadth of the room, eyes narrowed at the heavy oaken door leading out. Beyond it, faint voices pricked at his ears. Part of his skin-brother's pride was near. His crew. Darke growled at the snippets of the MC's inner cats' near-unintelligible murmuring punctuating the two-legged babble. That he could understand the crew's stupid yapping better than his own brethren's yowls irked.

A pang of loneliness shot through Darke's chest. He missed Clay. When his father's inner lion had spoken, his deep rumble was clarion. The lynxes out there? Yowls and hissing, Darke could pick out maybe one hard-won word in six, and they couldn't understand him at all. It had been the same with his littermates, Grapple and Shiv, leaving Darke to rely on instinct when forced to interact.

It got him in trouble. Lynxes were shady and two-leggers lied. Said things they didn't mean, then hurt you. Clay had been different, but he was dead while his murderer walked free.

Reaper.

Darke shivered, ears flicking back, remembering the bad time. The man who called himself their uncle needed to die, and Grapple and Shiv with him.

Darke's temper spiked, his tail swishing. Keenly feeling the loss locked within his mind again, in this stinking place of undead. His skin-brother shared his sorrow at their father's murder, but not Darke's isolation.

And now Grim had left him, too.

Darke shouldered through another door into a smaller room lined with tile. It smelled faintly of excrement and strongly of fabricated pine, the water in the bowl stale and chemical-laced. Darke shook droplets from his maw and chuffed his distaste, returning to the window.

Soft footfalls approached from the beyond the oaken door.

Darke slunk into the deep shadow of an armoire as the heavy slab canted open, then closed. Kit limped to the center of the room, favoring a leg. Her arm was splinted, the opposite hand bandaged in gauze. A ruddy stain marred its whiteness. She wrapped her damaged limbs around herself with a low sob, the scent of fresh blood perfuming the air as she moved. Darke's nostrils flared at that thread of wrongness twining within the delicate tendrils of citrus, cinnamon, and female musk.

His mate was presenting as wounded prey.

Darke bit back the growl building in his chest, fury pounding through his temples. His claws extended and retracted from the carpet's thick pile. Healthy, she'd be a tempting prize for any predator. Injured… He was going to kill—

No. Darke's ears flattened against his skull. His man would think before spilling blood.

But Grim thought too much.

Kit scanned the room, then dashed a hand across her face, stumbling to the bed. Her feet froze at its foot, head snapping toward the bathroom, then away. Another low sob eked from her throat, and Darke's ruff stood on end. He would destroy them. Destroy them all. Starting with those that had failed to protect—

—*Hey! Boy Vengeance! You really just gonna let her think her think he's gone?*—

Darke jumped, fur bristling at the syrupy censure. He backed deeper into the shadows, eyes wide and pulse pounding.

—*Aww. Here puss, puss, puss… I don't bite…*—

His lip curled over a canine, and a female's mocking laughter flitted through his mind as clearly as the gravelly chuckle of Clay's beast had. Darke's heart leaped, his ears pricking forward, saliva pooling in his maw.

He could understand her.

The beast inside Kit, his promised mate—when she spoke, her words were clear, and she wanted to *play*.

Shit. She wanted to play. He sent his consciousness back to his man, nosing at his inert presence. Shit, shit, shit… what should he do? Act cool. Grim would tell him to act cool. Not to screw this up. Game. *It's a game.* He knew how to play games… Darke buried his eagerness, narrowing his eyes and idly grooming a paw.

—*Oh, come on!*—

Seconds ticked by, then a frustrated huffing filled his mind.

—*Darke, please!*—

He lapped between his toes, blood pounding through his skull. Don't fuck this up, don't fuck this up—

—Listen, asshole, Kit's about to lose her—

Darke yawned. *—you are?—*

—Oooh! I'm about to kick your furry—

He sent her a visual of exactly how that would turn out. *[FURIOUS BLUSHING]*

Didn't fuck it up. Pleased at her reaction, Darke licked his chops, sauntering into the moonlight dappling the room as Kit placed a trembling hand upon the bed's rumpled covers. He froze mid-step. This game with his mate aside, Grim had warned him not to frighten Kit. How—?

—Don't stop now; rub up on her. Gently. Let her know you're here.—

Darke swallowed and pressed his brow to the small of Kit's back, chuffing.

She stiffened. Her scent subtly altered, a sour note of fear curdling through it. "G-Grim?"

—Do it again— his mate urged.

Darke butted against Kit, and she swayed, gasping.

—Now look cute.—

Teeth bared, his ears flicked back. *—cute?—*

—laughing—

Kit slowly turned, and Darke sat, forcing his anxiety to boredom, gaze on her throat, fighting the urge to lick his lips at the jump of her pulse.

—Dayum, that ain't cute, but not actively murderous works. How you're even finer on four legs…—

Darke chuffed his pleasure, pressing his head to Kit's abdomen and greeting his mate within. Her fingers sank into the soft fur below his jaw, and he leaned into her touch—

Moisture stained Kit's cheeks, salt tinging the air. Her fingers stiffened, and she sat back on the bed, her expression hard.

Had he done something wrong? Darke tensed, pulse hammering, waiting for the blow of her fist—

—*Shhh, Pussycat. This isn't about you. Give her a minute*— His mate's voice slid through his mind, its caress smoothing the edges of his fear. —*She's straight-up pissed at not having a choice in any of this. Pay attention, 'cause we got issues with overbearing males.*—

Darke heard the warning, but was pretty sure she didn't mean him. He butted against her, his ear turning back as he rubbed his face against her chest, releasing calming pheromones. Kit's brow furrowed and then she shivered, her body relaxing.

—*Mmm... Have I told you you're my new favorite smell? Do that again*—

The end of his midnight-tipped tail flicked against the carpet in amusement, and Kit's eyes caught his. His focus stole past their surface to her inner beast staring back at him. Darke's head cocked. It wasn't a challenge, more like...

An overwhelming sense of her loneliness washed over him. His mate knew his pain and shared it. She understood.

Kit dropped to her knees, pressing herself against the short, thick fur of Darke's chest. Her arms encircled his neck, and she gave a contented sigh. He snuffed at her hair, nosing it aside, his tongue rasping against her cheek.

She pulled back to meet his eyes again. "Is he okay?"

His man. Grim. Darke's muzzle crinkled, trying to send out his thoughts to her as he had with Clay, and met resistance. What—?

Darke's heart sank. Reaper's saliva hadn't triggered her change. His mate still wasn't free, and that loneliness he'd felt...

—*you hide*—

—*She's not ready.*—

He stared at his mate within Kit's eyes, and she looked

away at his censure, leaving him caught in Kit's warm chocolate gaze. *—tell her he heals—*

His mate paused, as if unsure, then, *—He'll be fine, Kit. Darke's got it handled, and until then, we got you, girl.—*

Kit's expression pinched closed, and a sob caught in her throat. Something like the buzzing of bees buffeted against his consciousness.

His mate replied to it, any earlier trepidation replaced with sass. *—Mmm… let's go with willfully ignorant and stubborn as hell. That's gotta change, along with this two-legged bullshit, and daddy dearest's deposit ain't done dick in that department.—*

Kit's hand rose to her throat, eyes wide with panic, but Darke didn't sense any argument from her. He yawned, pleased his mate had taken her two-legged skin-sister well in hand.

His attention returned to the man healing within their shared consciousness. When Grim woke, Darke vowed to do the same. There would be no more waiting.

It was time to claim their mate.

CHAPTER ONE

KIT BIT down on the inside of her cheek, one stiff breeze from totally losing her shit.

That inner voice she'd heard for as long as she could remember was her goddamned cat? How was that even possible? Shit wasn't supposed to happen unless she'd been exposed to a shifter's body fluids, and Reaper hawking into the back of her throat aside, she'd been so damned careful…

—It's different for queens— her cat said *—But just so we're clear, ain't nothin' about this new. I've been kickin' around since Billy Jenkins spit in your Kool-Aid at the third grade picnic. —*

Wait, you—and you're just telling me this now?! Kit got the distinct impression of a shrug. By the window, Darke put his back to them and began grooming himself with all kinds of "I'm staying the hell out of this" vibes. Smart cat.

Kit's kept going. *—All that shit that went down with Reaper wasn't the only reason Claymore got your ass out of Flatts. We were good until you started going to Community. That red-headed polo geek in your finance class? Trust me, you do not want to know what he put in your latte during midterms. You're lucky I clued you into how funky it smelled.—*

Argh! Kit raked a hand through her hair. *Are you fucking serious?*

—Deathly, and that ain't even half of it, girl. Since then, it's been a full-time job dodging shady shifter shit until we hooked up

with our mate. Trust me, Auntie Jojo wasn't a fucking prize, but Claymore's cat was right; she kept us clear of the bulk of those fuckers.—

Kit's jaw hung open. What? Her Auntie Jojo was a bible thumping species purist that'd looked down on Kit ever since she'd landed on her doorstep, and that fucking private human boarding school Claymore had somehow weaseled Kit into was the most miserable—

Hold up. What do you mean, Claymore's cat was right? The one and only time Kit had seen Claymore's beast was the night her mother had been shot, and it sure as fuck hadn't spoken.

—Look...you're not gonna be happy about this, but they had a plan for us—

A plan, huh? And how the fuck would you know that?
[GUILT]

—I might've spoken to his cat whenever Claymore checked in—
Kit saw red.

—but it's not like you and me were cool yet, so—
Nope. And we sure as fuck aren't now.

—Oh, come on, girl. Don't—

A knock on the door echoed through the room, and Darke was at her side in one sinuous motion, teeth bared.

Kit took a deep breath and wiped her eyes. *Dear Lord above, tell me this is not happening. It's too much.* It was all too damned much. How the hell she hadn't figured out that inner voice was her frickin' cat—And the furry bitch had been fucking conspiring against her with Claymore's goddamned beast? Ugh! Stupid, stupid—

The knock came again. "Katherine?"

Mr. Asorav. Damn it. Considering the vamp had saved all their asses by offering them a place to lie low after Club V had exploded, she probably shouldn't tell him to fuck off... but God frickin' damn, she wanted to.

—snickering—

Shut the hell up. "One a sec." Kit smoothed her hands over her cheeks, knowing it was pointless. If a vamp could target some poor fool's heartbeat a city block away, he'd definitely heard her crying. Whatever. Forcing a smile, she opened the door. "Yes?"

"I—" The ancient vamp's brows knit with concern as his gaze swept over her, all agitated in his Armani. "You haven't eaten, so I've taken the liberty of having a meal prepared for you." He scowled down at Darke. "And the cat."

Kit swallowed, ill at the thought of food. "Thank you, but I'm really not—"

"But the beast is. I can hear his stomach churning clear across the flat, and I doubt he'll leave your side." Darke chuffed his agreement from beside her, and Mr. Asorav grunted. "As I suspected. Shall we?"

Shit. Her mouth went dry at the realization she'd been in a room with a hungry two-hundred-pound-plus predator and was about to go to dinner with another. Kit re-plastered a smile on her face. Nothing to do but play it off. She took the vamp's proffered arm, ignoring Darke's low growl as he padded after them. Great, he sounded jealous. How the hell did she get herself into these situations?

—Oh, please. Asorav won't risk upsetting his dog by draining you dry, and Darke'll get over it. He's just a big—

Did I ask for your input? she snapped.

—Kit, I—

Back it up, bitch. You drop all that shit on me and think I'm just gonna roll with it? I don't even know your damn name.

[CHAGRIN]

—It's Kat—

Well, that's fucking original. Claymore come up with that, or was it all you? You know what, don't tell me. Doesn't matter, cause we not talkin'. Ow. Kit rubbed her temples. It was like she was using a totally different part of her brain to talk to the furry bitch, and damn, it sucked.

"Are the pain meds wearing off?" Mr. Asorav asked, slowly escorting her down the hall to accommodate how beat to shit Kit was.

She went to answer, but voices spilled out from the dining room ahead. *Fuck my life.* Grim's crew was still at the table. Kit glanced back at Darke. The big cat lagged behind them, and she got the feeling he wasn't looking forward to seeing them either. Weird. She shook her head and turned to the vamp.

"No, I'm good. Today has just been a lot."

"Indeed." They passed the threshold into the dining room and conversation stopped.

Grim's crew from the MC that'd ridden down with them for the moot ringed a table scattered with the remains of a meal. They were all still filthy, their cuts coated in a fine layer of grit from the explosion at the club.

None of them would meet her eye.

Well, except for the MC's massive enforcer, Brick. He grinned at her, continuing to rhythmically flick his switchblade open and closed, the snick counting down the seconds till she lost her shit.

Yeah, that was gonna happen sooner than not.

Mr. Asorav patted her arm again, leading Kit across the intricate mosaic floor to an empty chair at the long mahogany table. Doc hissed something at Brick, and he laughed, putting his fucking knife away.

"It's been some time," Mr. Asorav said, ignoring the byplay and pulling a heavily carved seat out for her, "but I do recall things being easier to face with a full stomach."

"Thanks, I—"

Darke stalked from the hallway, scowling, his shoulders bunched.

The tension in the room skyrocketed, everyone at the table going stock-still, eyes following the massive cat's every move. The tap of his claws against the tiny tiles was way louder than it should've been. He glowered at the crew; the light from the wall sconces throwing his facial markings into relief, the suggestion of a skull now stark.

—Dayum, that boy just gets finer…—

They're terrified of him. Kit swallowed the abrupt lump in her throat, totally forgetting she wasn't on speaking terms with her cat. Wrench, Deuce, Stitch… even Doc; they were all Grim's friends. His crew. *Why would they be afraid of his cat?*

—Mmm. It sounds like our boy's got anger issues and is seriously jacked.—

What do you mean?

—Mountain lions aren't supposed to be that big, and I can hear them. The crew's cats. They've all gotten into it with Darke…— Kat paused like she was listening. *—They're worried he's gone feral again.—*

Grim had said something about that. How his cat had taken over and wouldn't let him shift back to two legs. *Is that what happened?*

Kit winced at the distant hiss of static in her head, and things clicked. That had to be Kat talking to Darke, and whatever she was saying, he wasn't a fan. The big mountain lion growled low in his throat, and the crew tensed up. Brick's hand edged toward his gun.

Holy shit.

—He's not feral. Grim was in a bad way. Shifting lets him heal faster, and he wanted Darke to protect us… Kit, he can't understand them like I can. It's like him and the crew are speaking totally different languages. I think that's why he swings his dick around. The crew's cats confuse him.—

Fan-fucking-tastic. Kit pinched the bridge of her nose. Whatever. She wasn't getting involved. *And neither are you. Don't say a fucking word to any of them.*

[ACQUIESCENCE]

Darke stopped at Kit's side, his muzzle pushing up under her arm. Kit's fingers sank into the silken fur behind his ear before she thought better of it, and his chest rumbled as he leaned into her.

Jaws dropped, and Stitch swore, fumbling for his vape.

—*Haha. Now they're the ones confused.*—

Mr. Asorav cleared his throat, and Kit's cheeks heated. She sat. Darke's paw hooked around the chair beside her, swiping it to the floor and batting it away. Kit bit back a smile. Kat might be on to something with that swinging dick comment.

The vamp rolled his eyes and sighed, motioning to a servant. "If you would, Daniel?"

A gaunt vamp collected a silver tray heaped with meat from the sideboard and set it on the floor with shaking hands. Darke's stomach rumbled, but he ignored the offering, intent on another liveried minion that'd appeared to place a covered plate in front of Kit.

Her breath caught as he removed the lid. Soft-shell chicken tacos.

Darke growled, and the retreating servant's footsteps sped. Kit placed a hand on the big cat's shoulder, blinking away her threatening tears and not even caring how Mr. Asorav knew what her go-to comfort food was. She was just so frickin' grateful...

Tell Darke it's okay.

That weird static pricked at the edge of her consciousness again, and Darke relaxed, still ignoring his meal. Kit eyed his platter of meat. Had to look damn good to a hungry carnivore. If the amount of crimson pooling beneath the haunch was any indication, whatever it was had just been offed in the next room. The rumble of Darke's stomach cut through the silence again.

Why isn't he eating?

Kat preened. —*He says, ladies first.*—

Okaaay... Kit picked up a taco and took a bite. Her moan of appreciation for the pico de gallo was totally inappropriate, but Darke chuffed his approval and bowed his head to tear into the haunch. Those jaws... they effortlessly ripped the meat from bone. He peeled a long thin strip off and flipped the bloody cut at her plate, scarlet spatters and a rapidly spreading crimson pool seeping across the formerly crisp white linen.

"Fascinating."

Kit glanced at Mr. Asorav, seated a few chairs away. A low growl started in Darke's chest, his upper lip twitching at the vamp.

"Yes, yes, *cat*," Mr. Asorav said, waving away Darke's murderous glare like a bad smell. "You've made your intentions clear. I only meant that one hears tales of your rites, but seeing them play out is most intriguing. Be assured I have nary an untoward design upon Katherine." The vamp smiled at her over the rim of his wineglass. It was definitely not filled with cabernet. "Please, proceed, my dear, and never mind the mess. My valet is somewhat adept at removing difficult stains."

Kit's throat bobbed. *I just bet he is.*

—Screw the linens and take a damned bite. It's important. Darke's declaring us his mate to his pride. You need to accept.—

Well, that would explain why every eye at the table was on her. Kit picked up her knife and fork, sweat pricking her scalp. She sliced into it and nibbled on a corner of the gory chunk. Still warm, the coppery tang woke something primal in her, and the entire forkful was abruptly in her mouth. Her inner cat purred, reveling in the mineral slide of flesh down their throat.

It should've been disgusting, but before Kit knew it, Darke's offering was all but gone, and she felt better than she had since the explosion. What the heck had that meat been? All her injuries had stopped aching, and the dull throb behind her eyes was gone. She wasn't complaining, but with her luck, it was probably unicorn or something. So much for the Endangered Mythos Act. She held out the last bite to Darke, and he nipped it from her fingers, his chest rumbling in satisfaction.

"Well, fuck me dead," Stitch muttered, lighting up his vape. "Never thought I'd see the damned day. Ladies and gentleman, Grimdarke has hisself a queen."

"No shit," Brick said, retrieving his beer and draining it. The behemoth tipped the empty bottle at her. "Your majesty."

Doc snorted. "Fine. She's the real deal if that pain in the ass cat's on board. First order of business, Queenie-pie needs to settle this shit show, since none of you dumb fucks will listen to me." The uber-bitch turned her icy green glare to Kit. "As of fifteen minutes ago, the media's fingered Grim for the Club V clusterfuck. Despite that making the explosion paranormal on paranormal crime and falling well within our jurisdiction, the witches have asked for human law enforcement's assistance."

Kit's fork clanged onto her plate. No frickin' way. That shit straight-up didn't happen.

Darke's head rose from his meal with a low growl, his jowls stained red and tail thrashing. Everyone froze again, and that static was at the back of Kit's head.

—*Oooh, girl, he is MAD. Whoever cum-slut is, she's on borrowed time.*—

Pretty sure that's Nikki... Kit tore off a bite of her taco and chomped on it. *Grim said she was blackmailing him, and when he ended it, she started spreading lies. That's why he submitted to that witch's spell at the moot that messed him up so bad. He was trying to clear his name.*

—*Mmm. Seems like someone's hellbent on making sure that doesn't happen.*—

Kat wasn't wrong. The oculus had proven Grim's innocence, but Club V had exploded before the council could report back their findings. Question was, why pin it on him? It seemed like an awful lot of trouble to go to just to keep him from becoming president of a frickin' biker club in east butt-fuck New York… Unless you were Reaper. Kit didn't put anything past her father. The man was batshit.

She wet her lips. "You think Reaper blew up the club?"

"Is wiping back to front a shitty idea?" Doc snorted. "But who the fuck knows. Coulda been him, the witches—"

"Shit don't have t'be mutually exclusive," Stitch mused, tapping his vape against his knee. "Both of 'em is ambitious, and Sama was a mite too keen t'detain Grim. I reckon him agreeing t'the oculus forced her hand."

Doc looked at him like he was crazy. "You honestly think the queen witch blew up her own sect on the fly?"

"I don't think it was a last-minute thing," Brick interrupted, scratching his massive jaw. "When I was leaving the main room to haul Grim's sorry ass out of there, I wasn't the only one making a beeline for the exits." His steely blue eyes flicked to Mr. Asorav. "I passed by more than one group of witches and vamps headed out. Stinks like a culling to me."

The vamp returned his stare, silent.

"A culling?" Kit asked.

Brick's eyes didn't leave Asorav's. "Yeah, when the head of a sect decides to nix anybody causin' trouble en masse. Way shit has been playing out with the council, Clay's murder… if the foo shits…"

"Look," Deuce said, breaking the mounting tension, "Regardless of who fucked who back there, Grim's the one taking it up the ass now. Question shouldn't be why, but what to do about it." He frowned at his bandaged hand, flexing it.

"Mr. Asorav, you're on the council and were in that room. Can't you clear Grim's name?" Kit asked the vamp, snagging another bite of her taco. She was enjoying it way more than she should be under the circumstances, but hello, *tacos*, and stress eating was kind of her thing.

Mr. Asorav frowned, picking a non-existence speck of lint from the sleeve of his suit. "Unfortunately, the vampires have made several rather restrictive pacts with the witches over the last several decades. The last shifter queen's untimely demise—"

"Execution, more like," Stitch interrupted, mid-drag on his vape.

Asorav's eyes flicked to him in annoyance and then back to Kit, not correcting the old man. "I'm afraid my coming forward would violate a recent mandate, and as for the rest of the council, those not dead are in hiding." He made a point of catching Brick's attention. "This power play goes far beyond Mr. James's innocence or guilt, and I'm not at liberty to disclose more than that."

Doc snorted, riffling a tatted hand through her bedraggled mohawk. "But you're willing to get us clear of the city and back to Flatts before the MC votes for prez tomorrow?"

Shit. Kit had forgotten about that. How would they elect Grim after all of this?

The vamp sucked in his cheeks with a slow nod. "Loopholes can be a powerful tool when exercised properly, madame. However, that particular opportunity is rapidly coming to a close. Once the sun rises, my offer will be null and void. I'll also add that I expect the human authorities to be knocking on my door well before then. I'd prefer not to compel them. There are those of my brethren who would delight in, how do you put it… ah, I believe it's referred to as 'throwing me under the bus,' should I misstep. Willfully violating the coven's terms would be a rather large faux pas on my part."

Translation: They needed to leave. Kit looked at the crew. "So what's stopping you from taking him up on his offer?"

"He's a vamp."

"Our bikes."

"He says you and Darke gotta stay."

"Okay…" Kit ticked off a finger. "First off, Mr. Asorav has been nothing but kind to me. If he says he'll get you clear, I believe he'll do it." She glanced at the ancient vampire. Grim had called him the Darkling and said he was the vampire queen's hitman, but he'd helped them.. That had to mean he had some kind of honor… at least, she hoped it did.

"Do you swear you'll get them safely back to the chapter house, with no ill-intent befalling them or repercussions to the MC for your help?" she asked, channeling her corporate accountant persona. Navigating all that tax law had to be good for something.

A smile tipped up the vamp's lips. "I do. Provided they're ready to leave within the next ten minutes. I can't guarantee their safety past that departure window."

"Fine, but what about our bikes?" Wrench asked, scrubbing at his face. The MC's mechanic had been silent up until now, and Kit was more than fine with that after the hillbilly bullshit he'd spouted about Chanté. Her heart lurched, wishing there was some way to know if her bestie had made it out of the club okay…

"Your motorcycles here will return to Flatts with you, and the van will follow. However, with the witches' plea for assistance, we've had to allow federal agents full access to Club V. I've no idea when or if the one you left there will be released."

Kit could tell the crew wasn't real happy about that, but it wasn't like they could do anything about it. Before someone pitched a fit, she moved on to the next item on her bullet list. "Okay… so now what's this about Darke and me having to stay?"

"As I mentioned earlier, my queen has requested you attend her, and Mr. James's visage has become somewhat famous. Getting the others out of the city will be delicate enough without adding his recent notoriety into the mix."

Kit looked around the table. "I still don't—"

"Grim's America's most wanted, and the city's on lockdown," Stitch muttered. "Cell towers is out, hard lines been cut… we ain't been able t'get through t'the MC t'tell 'em this whole thing's a fuckin' smear job."

"His pic is all over the news, Kit. On two legs and four," Doc added. "Those markings of his ain't easy to miss, and they've put out an order to shoot on sight."

To shoot on sight? "But why? I don't understand, I mean I know Nikki—"

"The club whore's slander is just a means to an end," Mr. Asorav said, pursing his lips. "Both you and Mr. James have a much larger role to play, and as I stated before, my queen has requested you call upon her. That is the main impetus for you remaining behind. Aryanna will be able to impart more details than I. After which, I will see that you're escorted wherever you may wish to go."

Kit bit at her lip, not liking the sound of that. Why wouldn't he just say he'd take them back to the chapter house?

"If we're all in agreement?" the vamp asked, pointedly looking at his heavy platinum wristwatch as he stood.

Loaded glances volleyed around the table.

"Me and Brick are staying," Deuce said as everyone rose to their feet. Beside Kit, Darke went still.

Stitch's brow quirked. "You two sure about that?"

Deuce nodded. "Yeah. Enough of you are going back to knock sense into the rest of the club, and everyone knows I'd lie my ass off for Grim, even if he was fucking guilty." He eyed the vamp. "With him out of commission, Kit's gonna need someone on two legs to have her back."

"What about you?" she asked Brick. Between that stupid knife clicking and him going for his gun, she didn't get the impression he was real fond of her or Darke.

—Darke doesn't like him either— her cat murmured.

Great. The frickin' Goliath in leather grinned down at her. "I wanna beat the shit outta something." He smirked at Darke and the cat snarled. "Better odds I get to do it here."

"Splendid." Mr. Asorav smiled, his teeth a titch too sharp. He motioned to a servant. "Shall we, then?"

"Not until I check those dressings," Doc snapped, glowering at Deuce and hefting up the med kit that never left her side. "Asshole will let himself go septic and a fat lot of good he'll do anyone then. Can't imagine Queenie over there's much smarter."

—Bitch.—

You mean uber-bitch.

—snickering—

Deuce rolled his eyes and obediently held out his hand for the shrew. Doc's lips were a thin white line as she unwrapped the mitten of bandages from his right hand…

She inhaled sharply.

A smooth, coin-sized scar the pink of recently healed flesh marred his palm. Wide-eyed, she flipped his hand over. The top was the same. "I-I don't…"

"Nice. I thought it felt better," Deuce said, planting a sloppy kiss on her temple. "You're a miracle worker, Doc."

Her brows knit, and she smacked him away. "It wasn't me, dumb ass, and shouldn't be fucking possible."

"Unless your true queen is awakening," Mr. Asorav said softly.

The crew turned to stare at him, and then at Kit. She swallowed the lump in her throat, resisting the urge to wave. Shit. Had the vamp been serious about all that earlier? Kit glanced at him, and he gave her a solemn nod, his words coming back to her.

…To each paranormal sect there can be only one true queen, Katherine. And despite your current affliction with humanity, for the shifters, you are it, or will be, once you embrace your dual nature…

Crap. It wasn't weird unicorn meat. Accepting Darke's offering had done this.

Her inner cat was smug. *—I told you it was important.—*

Quiet. I'm still mad at you, and this doesn't make it better.

Kit unwrapped the bandages from her hand. A few hours ago, it had looked like ground chuck where she'd mashed it into broken glass.

Now there wasn't a mark.

How?

"I'd advise all of you to keep Katherine's identity close to your chests until her transition is complete," Mr. Asorav said, his flinty gray eyes alight with an anticipation that made Kit's stomach churn. "Now, shall we proceed?" He held out a hand, indicating they should follow him.

The crew slowly complied, as if in a daze.

Kit could relate.

"This goes bad, it's on you," Doc muttered, shouldering past her to follow the vamp from the room. Darke growled at the severe woman, and she psh'd him, regardless of the bead of sweat tracking down her nape as she passed by. Kit buried a hand in his ruff, watching them file out.

Deuce came to stand beside her. She glanced over at him and then away. He was shorter and wider than Grim, and looked like someone had peeled him out of the pages of GQ and stuck him in a cut. Chestnut tousled hair falling over one eye, pin-straight roman nose, high cheekbones… Everything about him screamed "fuckboy." He ran a hand over his chiseled jaw, his dark gaze intent.

"Grim's my best friend. I've beefed with his cat, but me and mine'll put it aside. He'd want another set of eyes on you." He eyed Darke askance. "One that knows what the fuck is going on. We run into Reaper, or any of his crew, you'll need intel and someone who can hold a gun." He looked at his hand and flexed it. "Especially if this true queen shit is legit."

"And I'll keep his fucking cat in line," Brick added, joining them.

Man. He was a damned giant, and had obviously earned

his place as the club's enforcer. An ebony crew cut shadowed his tatted skull, part of one ear was missing, and his nose had definitely been broken more than once. He grinned at Darke's growl, a chunk of gold winking from the back of his mouth where a molar should be, and smacked a meaty fist into his palm. Kit bit back the urge to say something about it being clobbering time.

"Thank you," she sighed. That they didn't think much of Grim's cat was plain, but she'd take their offers for what they were. *What does Darke have to say about all this?*

—He doesn't like it.—

Well, there's a surprise.

Deuce grunted, shuffling his feet. "So... you and Grim, huh?" He shot her a goofy smile that was way too frickin' charming.

Kit rolled her eyes and was saved from responding by Mr. Asorav coming back into the room. He clasped his hands together, rubbing them. "Right, I'm afraid we've an issue."

Brick's grin widened. "Nice."

"My thralls report a sizable force of police vehicles headed this way. I believe it would behoove us to make an expedient departure," The vamp said, ignoring him. "Fancy a jaunt to Haemic? At this juncture, my queen's protection would be welcome."

Kit's mouth hung open and then snapped shut. A fucking force of police vehicles? It had taken three days to get a beat cop to her apartment after someone had broken in. This shit was getting deep, but hiding out at Haemic?

Maybe not the best idea.

—Like you've never wondered what really goes down at that sex club.—

Wanting to know and finding out personally are two totally different things.

—Chicken.—

Kit raked a hand through her hair, abruptly

understanding why Grim fought with his cat so much. Okay, so yeah, the prospect of checking out the most exclusive sex club in the Village and the queen vamp's rumored lair was tempting, but it was also fucking stupid.

Humans hung out there with the express purpose of hooking up with vamps. In exchange for a little blood, the sex was supposed to be off the charts amazing. Like, every last one of them thought they were getting the better end of the deal amazing… until they disappeared. Some came back with fangs, but most of them didn't come back at all.

And as far as the paranormals who walked through the doors? They fell into that latter category. Kit had heard shifter blood in particular was in high demand.

Both Brick and Deuce looked like the vamp had just asked them to sacrifice their firstborn… which she'd also heard was an actual thing there. Given their expressions, Kit figured it probably held merit.

Mr. Asorav laughed. "Ah, I see the club's reputation proceeds it. I assure you, we won't be going there to mingle. Aryanna's offices are just above the main floor. It would be unseemly to associate with your sect openly, given our arrangement with the witches. You've nothing to fear, and I swear to you; you will leave as you entered… but we need to go." He nodded to someone over her shoulder, and Kit turned. A servant held out Grim's jacket for her to put on over her borrowed sweats and trainers.

She slipped her arms in, frowning. Something about Mr. Asorav's wording wasn't doin' it for her. "Swear to me you're talking about our physical and mental states, not the door we used."

The vamp chuckled. "Ah, little princess, already playing the game, are we? It makes one wonder how adept you'll become if allowed to progress."

Yeah, that didn't give her warm fuzzies either. He put a hand on her back, ushering her from the room. The guys followed close behind. "A bit of advice; despite Claymore's service to her, Aryanna holds shifters in contempt. Her promise to protect you notwithstanding, if she sees you as a threat and a loophole presents itself, I can't promise you she won't take it."

No surprise there. Vampires weren't exactly known for being on the up and up. Kit frowned. "Do we really have to go see her?"

The vamp paused, as if mulling it over.

—*He's talking to someone mind to mind,*— her cat whispered like they were in danger of being overheard.

Wait, can they hear us?

—*I don't know. I can't make out what they're saying, but there's definitely something else going on.*—

Fan-fucking-tastic.

CHAPTER TWO

DARKE'S EYES narrowed as the vamp let out a long breath he had no business taking. The creature set his teeth on edge. Things that were dead should stay that way.

Asorav gave Kit a slow nod. "Yes, I'm afraid—"

He broke off, his head jerking to one side like he'd heard something. His lips pursed as he moved to a wall covered with huge, crudely carved panels stinking of well-managed rot. He pressed one of the relic's rosettes, and a section swung inwards. "Quickly now."

The vamp hurried into a stark room beyond. Kit followed, hugging herself as she crossed the threshold. Brick and Deuce trailed after her, swearing under their breaths. Darke hung back, the fur on his nape rising. He started forward, whiskers vibrating. A weird tang bled into the air. Something wasn't—

Electricity shot through him, and he yowled, careening through the doorway, his fur standing on end, claws raking across the floor as he skidded, fangs bared.

His eyes narrowed at Asorav, and a growl built in his chest. *—trick—*

"Fuck," Brick swore, going for his gun.

—Darke!— Kat snapped at him *—Stand the fuck down. Asorav's our only way out of here!—*

The ancient vamp sucked in his cheeks. "Are we doing

this here, then?" he sighed, motioning for one of his thralls to close the panel. "Very well."

—*Darke!*—

The *snick-snack* of Brick racking his gun echoed through the chamber.

Darke ignored it. He'd deal with the big man later. —*trick* — he growled back at his mate, crouching to spring.

—*That asshole's gonna shoot you, and Asorav's not tricking us in, he's keeping us safe!*—

"Whoa! Hold up," Kit said, glaring at Brick and stepping between Darke and the vamp. "Everybody calm the fuck down. What was that we stepped through? A spell?"

"No." Asorav loosened his cravat. "This room is cloaked by an artifact which prevents its detection by one's senses or by magical means." He sniffed at Brick. "And I can assure you, your assistance subduing the cat won't be necessary."

The MC's enforcer snorted back, his gun trained on Darke. "Keep telling yourself that. What d'ya think, Deucey? Fifty bucks Darke rips his fucking guts out before the vamp clamps onto his throat."

"Why the hell would I bet against a sure thing?" Deuce asked, racking his own piece and pushing Kit behind him. "Now, whether he'll go after us when he's finished with the fucker, that's fifty-fifty."

A grin sliced across Brick's face. "Yeah… put me down for 'I fucking hope so.' "

That was another sure thing. Darke's lip twitched up over his canines with a growl, eyes fixed on the lying vamp. Artifact, spell… Magic was magic and all of it was bad. The reek of it, old blood, and abject terror flavoring the barren space scalded the back of Darke's throat. His claws flexed, gouging the wood floor surrounding the low stone slab at the center of the chamber where the malaise emanated from.

—*Darke!*—

—*bad place*—

—Outside is worse. Please, stand the fuck down!—

Kit peeked around Deuce, her face pale. "Why is Darke freaking out?"

"Apparently," Asorav said, "Mr. James's recent brush with magic, has resulted in him becoming over-sensitized to it. I can assure you, had I known that to be the case, I would have given fair warning, and won't make that mistake again. Now, our time is limited. Shall we settle this pissing contest?"

—See? It was an accident. Now stop and use your damned head. You can make him more dead later.—

Darke's ear flicked back at his mate's words. Grim would tell him to think too. If he went at the vamp, Kit could get hurt, and that would be bad. Besides, Kat hadn't said he couldn't put down the vamp, just that he had to wait… He chuffed, not liking this thinking thing. *—later?—*

His mate sighed. *—Yeah, Boy Vengeance. As in, after we're free and clear of this shit storm.—*

He shot Brick a side-eye. *—him too?—*

—We'll talk about it.—

Talk. Darke's ears flicked, not sure he liked that either. He chuffed again and sat, grooming his fur back into place. The last time he'd felt anything like that zap had been when Grim had been tased.

It had been a lot funnier then.

On the other side of the room, Deuce exchanged a look with Brick. The smaller man shrugged, holding out his hand. The enforcer frowned, re-holstering his gun, and took out his wallet. The buzz of their cats talking as he counted out bills was an unwelcome undercurrent in the back of Darke's skull.

Kit glanced at him and bit back a smile.

He licked down another errant patch of fur.

"I'll take that as a reprieve," Asorav said, moving farther into the room. He murmured something, and a door appeared where one hadn't been an eye-blink ago. A fluffy rat wearing a sparkly collar wriggled through, and the vamp snatched it up, crooning at it.

The chamber beyond was filled with electronics like the basement of the clubhouse, but had more flatscreens on the walls. A plush leather couch was directly opposite the largest, with one of those little refrigerators and a microwave at an end. Asorav went over to a computer, holding whatever the hell that wriggly thing was in one hand and typing with the other.

Deuce laughed. "Holy fuck, Mouse would lose his shit if he saw this setup."

"Mouse?" Kit asked, settling on the edge of the couch.

"The MC's tech nerd," he replied, grinning at her. It slid off his face when one of the screens flickered to life, showing the building's lobby and stairwells.

Armed men swarmed the lower levels, and dozens of them in tactical gear were working their way to the upper floors. Outside, the entire block had been cordoned off, news crews peppered amongst the gathering crowd. Deuce started pacing.

Darke's gaze slid over all of it, not caring, until it caught three figures sporting the long gray robes of the Blēda moving purposefully up the stairs.

Kit drew in a sharp breath, and her fingers buried in Darke's ruff. "The witches sent a triad of Blēda? But Sama was there when the council cleared Grim—"

"As I said earlier, this goes far beyond his innocence or guilt, but with the damage the oculus inflicted upon him… I thought we had more time before she made her move," Asorav murmured, his teeth worrying his lip as he transferred files on another screen. "Apparently, the witch queen isn't taking any chances with Mr. James. I'm not sure my artifact will be sufficient with their ilk present."

"What the hell is that supposed to mean?" Darke's ears flicked back at the note of hysteria in Kit's voice. I didn't seem to bother anyone else. She looked between them. "How are we gonna get out of here?"

"Through them sounds good to me," Brick said, dropping the magazine in his gun to check the ammo.

"I wouldn't suggest it." The vamp rifled the fuzzy thing's fur. "But, that is the question, isn't it? I'd hoped for you to wait them out in here, but with a triad's involvement... I'm afraid my typical means of departure won't suit, unless perhaps your gift is turning people to mist?" he asked Kit.

She glowered at him.

"Pity," Asorav sighed. "Then your only option is the carrion chute in the other room."

Deuce stopped pacing. "The fuck is a carrion chute?"

"Exactly what it sounds like." Asorav eyed the screen once more before entering a line of code and powering it off. "Come, we've little time."

They followed him back to the other room. The vamp knelt and pushed the slab on the floor to one side. The putrid stench of decay wafted up, and Darke sneezed, the fur on his nape rising.

—bad place— he growled.

For once, his mate didn't have anything to say.

"Jesus fuck!" Deuce backed away, pulling his shirt up over his nose. "You want us to go down there? Are you out of your fucking mind?"

"It's either that or be subjected to the Blēda's tender mercies." The vamp gave a slow nod at their silence. "As I thought. The chute should be relatively free of impediment, but it empties into the sewers... the old sewers that drain into the Hudson. There are things down there better left to themselves."

Deuce ran a hand up the back of his neck. "I dunno... the shit I've heard—"

"If Mr. Asorav says this is the only way, it's the only way," Kit said, looking a lot less confident than she sounded.

—?—

We can't stay here…

The vamp tipped his head at Kit. "Quite. As I was saying, once down there, keep to the right branching tunnels. When you reach the lobby, take the middle lift. I hope to catch up with you before then, but should I be delayed… Aryanna is… sensitive about her appearance. You'd be wise not to remark upon it. And Kit?"

"Yeah?" She'd retrieved her scarf from Grim's jacket and tied it so she could pull it up over her nose.

"Be a dear and take Cecelia, won't you?" He held out the furry rat, and it yipped, tongue lolling. She looked at him like he was crazy. "Mr. Asorav, I'm not really sure—"

"I am," he said, forcing it into her arms. "I don't see this ending well, and I'd prefer to go out there knowing Cecelia's in your care. The little darling has my heart, and I trust you to keep her safe."

Kit bit her lip and reluctantly nodded, tucking the fuzzy rat into Grim's jacket and zipping it up. "I'll do my best."

Darke swallowed a growl, weirdly jealous.

—Think of it like packing a snack— his mate said dryly.

He perked up at that, licking his chops.

Asorav glanced at Darke askance. "Splendid, now, I'd suggest Sergeant Arroyo go first."

Brick shot him a foul look and moved to stare down the rancid hole. "This looks like a straight fucking shot, and we're on, what? The twentieth floor?" His eyes brightened and a deranged grin spread across his face.

"There's a short drop and then it curves to follow the building's exterior." Asorav explained. "Though steep, I assure you, it's entirely possible to survive."

The enforcer sat at the edge, dangling his legs, and rubbed the dark stubble peppering his jaw. "You said the sewers. M' I gonna land in shit?"

"Not at all."

"Dirt?"

"There's a pool."

"Nice." Brick grinned at him like he'd just given him season tickets, then pushed off, disappearing into the chute. A faint "Hooah!" echoed up in his wake.

The vamp's eyes glittered, turning to the rest of them with a smile that made Darke's ruff stand on end. "Who's next?"

"JESUS FUCK. I can't believe I'm doing this..." Deuce took a deep breath and dropped into the chute, following Brick down.

The vampire chuckled, turning to Kit and offering his hand. "I believe it's your turn, my dear."

Right. Yeah. Her turn. Her fingers shook as they found his cold, dry palm. He patted her arm. "I'll join you as soon as I'm able. Until then, follow my directions implicitly." He helped her to the edge of the gaping hole. "Don't dally by the pool, and it would behoove you to refrain from bleeding while you're down there. That will draw the wights like naught else."

Kit tensed against his hand on her back. "Wait, wights—"

The vamp gave her a shove, and she was falling.

Kit's eyes went wide, inhaling to scream as she plummeted, her arms squeezing the tiny dog to her chest. Cecelia yelped, trying to squirm away. The Pomeranian sent up a howl as they hit an angle in the chute, careening in a different direction. It knocked the breath from Kit, her shoulder throbbing as they sped through pitch-black darkness. The back of Grim's jacket rode up and sticky filth she probably didn't want to think about too much slicked over her skin.

They hit another jag. Kit yelped at the impact, tucking

herself into a ball around the frantic dog. "Shhh, shhh, shhh… it's okay…"

—*Girl, who the fuck are you tryin' to convince? Not one fucking thing about this is okay! That asshole just pushed us to our fucking deaths!*—

A yowl and the long screech of claws on metal sounded behind her. Darke. The hair on Kit's nape rose. *Didn't you just convince me to tell the others this was a good idea?* She yelped, her hip smashing against the chute's side with another change in direction.

—*This is not the time to play the who was right game, Katherine.*—

Kit laughed. *Are you for real? Speeding down a fucking death spiral you gave the green light to is exactly the fucking*—

The surface beneath her disappeared, and Kit was falling.

She drew a breath to scream and splashed into foul, icy liquid. Her arms flung out to the sides, hands battering against sharp angles—she grabbed onto something, eyes burning. A foulness invaded her mouth and nose, her stomach clenched—

A hand grabbed Grim's jacket, yanking her upwards.

She thrashed against it, breaking the surface with a heaving gasp as she was hauled onto solid ground. Kit fell to her knees, pulling her sodden scarf down and retching. Everything she'd ever eaten came up and then some. *Ugh, God… Where were*—A cavern. She was in a cavern by a pool of foul she didn't know what, everything lit by weird green light—

Including an arm, its putrid, decaying flesh clenched in her hand.

She shrieked, falling back and kicking it into the pool.

Oh God, Oh, God—

"Easy, easy, Kit. Shit's fucking nasty, but it ain't gonna kill you… Well, not right this second, at least. Dunno about the dog, though."

Deuce. She panted, wide-eyed, staring at the pool's settling surface. Deuce had pulled her out of whatever that was. Oh God, what the hell was that? Kit gagged, spitting vomit from her—

Oh no.

Cecelia. Shit. She'd lost hold of Mr. Asorav's dog…

"Here." Brick handed her a two-pound ball of nasty sopping fur. The guys didn't look any better. Both of them were drenched with whatever was in that pool, the white of their eyes and Brick's grin ghoulishly stark against faces streaked with filth. What the fuck was he so happy about? She didn't even want to think about what she looked like. What was in her hair—

Her stomach clenched again.

—Yeah, don't think about that.—

Fuck you. After this, dealing with one of the Blēda sounded pretty fucking good. Kit's brow furrowed, concentrating on the bedraggled Pomeranian. Cecelia's pristine white fur was a horrible ruddy brown, and she was barely—

The screeching from the chute abruptly ended and a massive wave of foul liquid shot up from the pool, drenching them again.

Oh, sweet baby Jesus—Darke.

A frantic torrent of filthy water doused the cavern, bombarding them with a deluge of shit she knew she didn't want to see. It hit the stone around them with horribly wet squelching thunks and the clatter of bone. The men swore, and Kit covered her head, scooting backwards over the cavern's gritty floor. Ugh, the fucking smell… Her spine hit the wall, and she whimpered, just wanting it to stop.

Claws scrabbled over stone and a Godawful yowl tore through the air. Another round of spatter sprayed over them.

"Jesus fuck, cat!" Brick yelled.

Kit peeked over her knees. Darke stood at the edge of the pool, legs splayed and panting. His expression was straight-up fucking murderous. He sighted Kit and shook himself again, jiggling his paws as he stalked forward. The big cat paused mid-step, an ear cocking backwards. He turned to face one of the tunnels on the other side of the pool with a low growl building in his chest.

—He says we need to move, something's coming.—

A laugh burbled up Kit's throat. Something was coming. Of course there was. She clambered to her feet, knees knocking and back scraping against the wall. Chunks of iridescent green slime and lichen landed at her feet amongst the gory detritus of the pool.

It was like she was standing in a corpse salad. Did that make her the protein add-on?

—Girl, you need to keep your shit together and head down that tunnel on the right.—

The guys must've picked up on whatever Darke had heard. They'd stepped up to flank him, and Brick's gun was in his hand again. Would it even work after that?

He caught her side-eyeing it and grinned. "S'a Glock, babydoll." He kissed the barrel. "Tank can roll over one of these beauties, and it'll still fire."

Good to—

The ground rumbled above them, dirt sifting down.

"Right, that's our fucking cue." Brick sent a kick in Darke's direction. "Move, cat. You got the best eyes down here, that puts you on point."

Darke swung around hissing, and the enforcer jumped back with a laugh. The cat chuffed at him and stalked to the tunnel.

—Boy Vengeance is not a fan.—

Boy Vengeance? Kit asked, following after him. She tucked Cecelia into the inside pocket of Grim's jacket beside his wallet and a soggy manila envelope. Hopefully it wasn't anything important.

Deuce and Brick trailed behind her. An awful groaning

filled the air, and the cavern shook violently, rocks smashing into the pool. The four of them sprinted through the tunnel's opening, the rumble from above like a freight train bearing down on them. Whatever was happening up there with the Blēda didn't sound like it was going so hot. Kit said a silent prayer that Mr. Asorav would be okay.

—He'll be fine. Man's a bad ass vamp.—

A massive crack shot through the air and a cloud of grit exploded from behind Kit. She fell to the ground coughing, the low light from the walls snuffed.

—Goddamn, you shoulda said your prayers for us.—

"Wooo!" Brick laughed. "Shit just keeps getting better."

"You're hard right now, aren't you, you sick fuck," Deuce grumbled, coughing as he spat.

A V of light flooded the tunnel. Brick held a little flashlight beneath his chin, grinning. The air around them sparkled with settling particulate, covering them with fine gray silt wicking to gory mud as soon as it landed.

"You know it, brother." The enforcer shifted his cock and winked at Kit.

Great. Nothing like being trapped underground with a pervy adrenaline junkie, a pissed off mountain lion, and a fuckboy. She tugged her scarf back up around her nose. It was frickin' nasty, but kept her from breathing dirt. Darke butted against her, and she flinched at his matted fur.

Tell me he's not gonna lick that.

—No promises. He says whatever was behind us is still there. We gotta bounce.—

Kit struggled to her feet, eyeing the flashlight. "How the hell does that thing even work?"

"With batteries." Brick said it like she was an idiot.

"It's waterproof," Deuce amended, elbowing him in the gut. "Psycho's ex-Army. Asshole probably has MREs and a tent shoved up his ass," he muttered, rising to his feet and wiping his hands on his jeans. "Fuck, that's nasty."

Whelp, at least one of them was prepared for this shit show. "Guess he's on point, then."

Brick grunted, pushing past them. The tunnel wasn't wide, his shoulders a hand's breadth from scraping the sides. They followed the big man down the sloping passage, the sounds of their footsteps too loud in the omnipresent silence. Kit shivered, dripping. Her sodden clothes dragged at her. It was definitely colder down here than it'd been at the pool. The tunnel branched and Brick headed down the right fork. Gradually, the air grew clearer. Kit dropped her scarf, wishing like hell she was anywhere else right now.

The walls of the offshoot they'd taken were smooth, and she caught glimpses of old tags on the wall, the paint muted shades of grays. Sections of brick held together with crumbling mortar came and went, and the distant sound of water running slowly intruded upon the eerie quiet until it was all she could hear.

Brick led them closer to it, down another branching tunnel. This one opened into a long arching brick vault, rank with sewage. Sludgy effluent splashed down from an open pipe at one end into a wide channel running down the room's center, then churned past a thick-barred gate where the room dead-ended.

They stood there, staring at it.

Shit.

CHAPTER THREE

DARKE SLUNK into the shadows of the vault, his eyes on the tunnel they'd just exited. The skittering that'd followed them from the pool was catching up. Pretty soon, the two-leggers would be able to hear it over the running sewage. He pawed at his nose, sneezing, and eyed the rest of the chamber. The filthy channel would keep them on one side of the vaulted room unless they went swimming again, but chances were good it would also slow down whatever was coming their way. He just needed to give Kit and those two fuckwits a reason to cross.

Hopefully there was one.

Darke bunched his legs and leaped to the other side.

"Did we miss a turn?" Kit asked. Her breath frosted around her face, her lips pale. They needed to get her some place warm. Darke snuffed at the vault's walls, sneezing again. There was a faint thread of something…

"Do I look like I miss shit?" Brick snorted, swinging the beam of light over the walls. He sighed and ran a hand up the back of his neck, muttering. "I don't miss shit."

"Can't when you're covered in it," Deuce deadpanned. "The fuck is the cat doing?"

The beam of light washed over Darke, and he growled at the loss of his night vision. Not that he needed it to know someone had come through here recently. Their trail ended abruptly at the far wall.

"Maybe he found a way out?" Kit asked, craning her neck to see what he was doing.

Brick put a hand to his ear and gasped. "What's that Lassie? Timmy's in a well?"

"No wonder Darke hates you." She scowled. "Can you be any more of a dick?"

Deuce groaned. "Please tell me you didn't just ask him that."

"Oh, but she did, Deucey, she surely did." Brick smacked the smaller man on the shoulder, making him stumble. "Challenge accepted."

Idiots. Darke stood on his hind legs, snuffing… One spot on the wall had layers of old smell, like it was a touchpoint. He raked a claw over it and chirped.

"Hah! See, I told you I don't miss—Shit, you hear that?" The flashlight's beam swept across the chamber to the tunnel, and Brick didn't wait for an answer. "Start climbing, motherfuckers."

"C-climbing?" Kit stuttered, hugging herself.

"Yeah, unless you wanna go bobbing for crap-ples." The flashlight's beam hit the gate spanning the channel of sewage. "Deucey, test it out. See the crossbar just under the surface? Stand on it and work your way across."

"Why the fuck do I have to be the guinea pig?" He winced, rubbing at his stomach.

" 'Cause it was my idea," Brick shrugged. "And it's a bad fucking time for tummy troubles, dude."

"Fuck you, my meds are with my ride." Deuce submerged a boot, scowling as he grabbed onto an upright bar and started across.

"You need medication?" Kit's brow furrowed. "Are you going to be okay?"

"He'll be fine," Brick snickered. "But his pants won't be."

"Shut it, asshole!"

"I'm not the asshole you need to worry about."

Darke bit back a chuff of annoyance at their banter. The scrabbling from the tunnel grew louder, and he padded closer, intent on its mouth…

The noise beyond stopped.

Darke crouched low, his hind quarters twitching.

"Do you have any fucking boundaries?" Deuce's boots hit the ground.

"Nope. Now catch Kit."

"What?"

"Wait—!" Her scream echoed through the vault, and a hunched form burst from the tunnel. Darke was airborne before it cleared the opening, slamming into it and skidding into the far wall. Putrid flesh squelched between his jaws, his claws rending across exposed bone. The thing screeched, its teeth sinking into Darke's foreleg.

He yowled, slashing back at it and going for its throat.

"Holy fuck, it's a goddamned wight!" Brick swore, jumping the last few feet from the gate to the other side of the channel and training his gun on it. "Figure out how to open that fucking wall before the rest of them show up!"

"The fuck do you think I'm trying to do, asswipe?!"

"Here," Kit yelled, "Darke scraped the wall here—"

Something metallic clicked, and wood rasped over stone.

Darke's jaws crunched down, shaking the foul creature. Globs of animated decay spattered across the surrounding brick. The wight screamed as its spine tore free, and Darke whipped the gory vertebrae into the channel, bounding after it. He launched over the divide and landed with a pained yelp on the other side, the poison from the creature's bite throbbing up into his shoulder.

"Hurry the fuck up, they're coming!" Brick yelled at him, his eyes on the tunnel. Darke ignored his encroaching tunnel vision and tore past him. The enforcer slammed the door shut, laughing manically when something slammed into it a second later. "Hahaha! Fuckers!"

Kit's anxious face peeked around Deuce as Darke skidded to a stop, panting. He shook his head, swiping a paw over his ear. A wave of nausea roiled through him.

—Dayum, Boy Vengeance, that was hot as fuck.—

Darke chuffed, his chest puffing up at his mate's reaction… or maybe he had to puke. He flopped onto his side, tongue lolling from his mouth and panting. *—protect you—*

That's right, anything tries to touch her, you fuck 'em up…

Darke's breath hitched, his eyes closing as he turned his attention inward.

Grim was awake.

Barely, buddy. That spell was no joke. His man winced. *Neither is that fucking bite. The fuck possessed you to tangle with a wight?* Grim's light pulsed, sending him strength as Darke tried to explain everything through the fog clouding his mind. *So let me get this straight. The witches are trying to pin everything on me, Asorav threw down with the Blēda, and now we're skulking through the sewers to get to a fucking audience with the vampire queen?*

—yes—

Grim grunted. *Goddamn… and Kit's beast can understand you?*

—yes—

Better work on stringing more than two words together then.

—fuck you— Darke grumbled, conceding that his man had a point. Females like talking. At least the two-legged ones never seemed to shut up.

Grim winced again as nausea roiled through them. *Wanna play a game?*

—a game?— Darke's ears half-heartedly perked forward.

Yeah. It's called don't let anyone know I'm awake yet.

The big cat chuffed. Why would Grim want to play dead?

—boring—

Won't be when we surprise all the fucks trying to kill us. It's... it's like a trick.

Darke's lip raised into a snarl. He didn't like tricks. If you were going to kill something, just kill it. Playing with it was different. Your prey still knew it was going to die, but that made it more fun. Besides, he didn't want to trick his mate. — *Kit Kat?*—

We'll tell them when we're out of here. I don't trust those fucking vamps. They're probably keeping tabs on us.

Darke didn't trust them either, for all Kit did. How they'd gotten her to do that was definitely some kind of a trick. A bad one. —*Brick?*—

Grim growled. *Asshole keeps manhandling Kit, and he's all yours... Until then, you need to get over his lynx getting the jump on you last time you two went at it.*

—*let him*—

Suure you did, buddy. Look, we'll tell him and Deuce, just not—

"Darke?"

At his name, Darke retreated from his mind. Kit's brows were knit as she stroked his head. He blinked, groggy, as he took in the new tunnel. All big wood beams and dirt, like a mineshaft.

Probably from prohibition.

Darke didn't know what Grim was talking about, or care, aside from the fact that one of those massive timbers had been wedged up against the door. Nothing would be following them for a while, despite the claws scrabbling at the other side.

Which explained why Kit's attention was riveted on him instead of running.

—*You good, Boy Vengeance?*— his mate asked. —*You went pretty deep there for a while... is it the bite? Looks nasty.*—

—*fine*— He absently licked his swollen foreleg and instantly regretted it. Tasted like death, and hurt.

—Mmmm—

"Hey Brick, you have anything on you for bites?" Kit asked, frowning at it.

"He got bit?" The two men exchanged a look. "Uhh… think it's kinda like a snake bite…" the enforcer said after a long pause.

Kit bent closer, her frown deepening. "Aren't you supposed to suck the poison out of those?"

"Whoa, wait, no, you don't wanna do that." Deuce pulled her back. "How about we just wrap it up until we can clean it or some shit?"

Her eyes narrowed. "What the fuck aren't you telling me?"

Before one of them could lie, Darke interjected, *—fatal—*

—WHAT?!— his mate screeched, and Kit burst into tears a moment later.

Darke sent her a mental shrug. He didn't feel like he was dying. At least, not anymore, but that's what he'd heard happened when one of those things bit you.

Dude. Not fucking cool. his man groaned. *You can't say that to her! Tell her you'll be fine. Probably. Have her wrap it up with the dick scarf. Kit'll like that.*

Darke huffed. He wasn't lying to her, but he supposed that last part would be ok. *—scarf?—*

The buzz of Kat relaying the message pricked at him, and Kit wiped her eyes, sniffling.

"Hey! Hey," Deuce crooned. "Maybe he'll be fine, considering all that healing mojo you did back at the vamp's flat."

She smacked him away from her, glaring as her fingers working at the scarf's knot.

"Yeah. Totally possible," Brick said like it wasn't. "But if you feel like wrapping your lips around something—"

"It'd be the barrel of that gun if you were my only other option," she snapped, cinching the nasty bit of cloth around

Darke's foreleg. He bit back a yelp at the jolt of energy that shot through him, his vision going white. "You two are assholes. He's gonna be fine."

—magic— Darke panted, his skin buzzing with it.

Yeah, we'll worry about that and Brick crossing the fucking line with Kit later. I told you it'd make her feel better. Now play it off.

—?—

Rub up on her and act grateful, you dumb fuck.

Darke bent his head and butted against her, releasing calming pheromones, and Kit sighed.

See? She bought it.

Kat didn't. *—Don't think I don't know what you just did there. Roofie her ass again, and Imma kick yours.—*

Darke chuffed at his mate's annoyance and wobbled to his feet. He didn't see the problem.

—Now that's exactly the kind of overbearing bullshit I was talking about.—

He bit at the scarf. The buzzing over his skin had become a concentrated itch. Beside him, Kit shivered, probably feeling the cold even more now that her adrenaline was crashing.

"How long have we been down here?" she asked, hugging herself. She didn't look like she was going to be able to go much farther.

Brick glanced at his watch. "Thirty-five minutes."

"That's it?"

"Yeah, but now that we're out of the sewer heading east at a positive grade, I'm optimistic about our ETA."

Kit blinked at him, and Deuce muttered something about PTSD.

"He means the tunnel's sloping up in the right direction, and dude, if you fucking wig out on me down here…" Deuce sighed, shaking his head, and snagged the light from the big man as he pushed past him. "We're in the fucking sewer, not the desert."

"Fuck you."

"Fuck all of this. Let's go. I need to find a goddamned bathroom."

***

KIT PINCHED across her temples before following Deuce, his arm pinned across his gut. Thirty-five minutes. How the fuck could it only be thirty-five minutes? She glanced back at Darke. His limp wasn't pronounced, but she could tell that bite was a lot more painful than he let on. Frickin' men.

Do you think he was serious about it being fatal? she asked her cat.

—Yeah, but I also think Deuce has a point about us healing them earlier. Girl, we were all fucked up over shitty and then boom, not so much.—

Kit bit back her tears. Then why hadn't Grim come back yet? She reached into his jacket to check on Cecelia, not wanting to think about it. Not that thinking about the little dog was much better. She hadn't stirred once since being dunked in that pool. Her breathing was regular, but she was out cold. Kit's stomach dropped. God, what would Mr. Asorav do if she had to tell him she'd killed his dog?

—Technically, he pushed us down that fucking chute, sooo—

Kit bumped into Deuce's back, cutting off her reply. He put a finger to his lips and switched off the flashlight.

The sudden plunge into pitch black softened to mottled gray as her eyes adjusted. Around a bend in the tunnel, a door was outlined in light. Darke pressed against her thigh, chuffing as he scented the air. She could just make out Deuce watching him in the gloom, then give a nod when the big cat chirped. Neither one of them moved forward.

"Oh, for the love of fucking—" Brick raised his gun and shoved past them, slamming his shoulder against the metal slab. It flew open and light poured into the tunnel. Kit held up a hand, blinking at the brightness. "It's the lobby Asorav was talking about," the enforcer called back.

"Well, that was anticlimactic," Deuce muttered.

"Aww…" Brick grabbed him in a headlock and riffled his hair. "Look at you, using big words. I'm so damned proud. Double points for being contextually accurate."

"Fuck you, dude," he growled, squirming away.

"If I swung that way, you'd be the first to know, Deucey," Brick said, winking at him.

Kit rolled her eyes, stepping into the lobby. Sconces with off-kilter beaded red shades lit the sad little room's worn, brown and red carpet and the mustard-colored wallpaper bubbling around the burnished double doors of three elevators. A strip of the hideous stuff dangled, flashing the garish green print beneath it, and partially hiding the call button for the middle elevator. Their doors were surprisingly beautiful; shadowed and embossed with geometrics like something straight out of the 1920s.

But the camera blinking at them from one of the corners was definitely up to date.

Brick shot it the bird.

Deuce laughed, then grimaced, clutching his stomach. "You're a fucking psycho."

"That's been medically disproven, I just really love my job." He grinned, tearing off the lolling strip of paper and jabbing that same finger at the elevator's call button.

"You're both out of your damned minds," Kit muttered, burying her fingers in Darke's sticky ruff to stop him from biting at her scarf. "Leave it alone."

—He says it itches.—

Good. That means it's healing.

Her cat snorted. *—You know that's bullshit, right?—*

Don't care. He's keeping it on. Beside Kit, Darke chuffed, giving her some serious side eye. "Oh, deal with it."

The elevator binged and the doors slid open. Brick shot

the camera another bird and stepped inside. Deuce gave a pained laugh, and Kit followed them into the wood-paneled box with Darke, cringing at the insipid music. A tired rubber plant was in one corner, its crackle-glazed pot overflowing with cigarette butts.

—*Damn, it's like a fucking coffin in here.*—

Kit frowned. *Thanks for that visual.*

The doors slid shut, and the elevator jerked, slowly rising.

"What number did you hit?" she asked Brick.

"Aren't any," he said, eyeing another camera. This time, his hands stayed firmly jammed into his cut's pockets. He started whistling off beat to the music.

After what seemed like an eternity of soft jazz, and Brick's terrible rendition of "Love in an Elevator," it jerked to a halt. Kit put out a hand to steady herself, and the doors opened.

—*Dayum.*—

Yeah. That… Kit gaped at the black mirrored walls with bold geometric overlays of gold that greeted them. Rectangular pillars of the same rose from a tawny sandstone floor. She wet her lips and ventured into an intimate sitting area. Purple velvet couches and brown suede bucket chairs were set to view the expansive skyline of the city through a wall of dusky windows. To the side, a gas fireplace burned, its blue flames licking over sparkling ebony stone.

No lie, the place was chi chi as hell, and didn't look like a club or an office.

A woman cleared her throat, and Kit turned as a slim brunette in a pantsuit stepped from the shadows. She smirked, her canines long enough to dimple her plump plum lips. Wherever they were, they'd been expected.

"Aren't you three a sight, but I suppose I shouldn't be surprised after the Darkling's earlier performance. It's a wonder you got here at all. Well, more of a pity really, but cockroaches are so difficult to kill."

Yep. They'd been expected, but definitely not welcome.

—*Bitch.*—

Darke growled, and Kit put a hand on him. *Tell him to play nice.* "Is Mr. Asorav okay?" she asked.

The vamp ran her sharp gaze over Kit like she was looking for something, and for whatever reason, Kit was abruptly certain that now would be a very bad time for Cecelia to wake up.

"The Darkling? I doubt it," the vamp said cheerfully. "He and that Blēda made a quite a mess of the city. My mistress isn't amused. It's called far too much attention to our sect, and given her no choice but to remand him into the witches' custody. They've detained him at the Spire."

Kit flinched. The Spire was a maximum-security paranormal prison. Well, as far as humans were concerned. The reality of the situation was much more final. "Is he, um…"

"Dead?" The vamp's dark eyes glinted. "Yes, for several centuries now, I'm afraid. Funny how that works."

Kit flushed. "No, I meant—"

"The term you're looking for is 'de-animated,' and unfortunately, without his heart, impossible." She looked none too pleased about that, then perked up. "Though, I'd imagine right about now he's very much wishing it was."

Kit's brow furrowed. Without his heart? What the heck did that mean?

"Right, don't give a shit," Brick said, leaning against a pillar. Gore scraped off his cut onto the wall's overlays. "Who the fuck are you, and where's the queen?"

"I'm Hillary Birch, the queen's amanuensis." The vamp sniffed, looking down her nose at him. "That's—"

"You take notes for her memoir. Got it," the big man said, bored.

Hillary's eyebrow rose, nonplussed. "The queen has been detained dealing with tonight's political fallout. The humans are none too pleased to have lost another chunk of their city.

She's bid me to offer you the use of her guest suite to freshen up whilst she deals with the matter."

"Bathroom?" Deuce gritted out.

The vamp's eyes slid over him, unimpressed. "Down the hall, second door on your right." He grunted, taking off in a running waddle. Brick laughed, and her gaze snapped to him. "If the rest of you will follow me?"

Hillary turned on her heel, not giving them a choice in the matter, her red-soled stilettos clacking smartly down the hall in the direction Deuce had gone. Guess they were following.

"The en-suite bath is just through there," the vamp said a few doors later, opening one and pointing through a lavish bedchamber of cream and rose at another opening. "A selection of clothing is in the closet for your perusal. I'll see that your companion joins you as soon as he's able. Please note the suite is sound-proofed. My mistress finds it inconvenient listening to minutiae whilst in her own home." A faint smirk painted her lips at an inopportune groan and splash from across the hall. "Unfortunately, the common spaces have not been afforded the same luxury."

"Dude, courtesy flush!" Brick yelled.

Kit smacked him, her cheeks burning hotter at the muffled, "Fuck you," from Deuce.

"What?" Brick asked like he didn't know. Kit's glare didn't seem to clear it up for him. "Fucker grew up in a barn. I'm trying to keep this shit civilized." He winked, puckering his lips and smooching them at the vamp.

She arched a brow, and Kit groaned, hand over her face. *Where the fuck was a rock to crawl under when you need one?*

"Should you require anything, feel free to use the intercom by the door and a thrall will attend to you," the vamp said, strutting off without a backward glance.

Brick elbowed Kit. "Think she's into me?"

"You keep it up, and her fangs will be, you idiot," Kit hissed, ignoring the frilly bedroom and heading for the en-suite bath. She wasn't thrilled with having to wait, but meeting the vampire queen covered in filth hadn't exactly been appealing, either.

The bedsprings squealed as Brick landed in the center of the cream lace bedspread, dirty as fuck with his nasty-ass still dripping funk. Kit's jaw dropped. He did not just do that…

Darke butted against the small of her back.

—*Girl, go take a shower.*— her cat said, agreeing with him.

Kit shook her head. Deuce was right. Man was a frickin' psycho.

Darke followed her into the bathroom, his claws tapping across the black-and-white checkered tiles. The vanity of ebony wood topped with gold-veined cream marble was tastefully loaded with every product Kit had ever dreamed of slathering over herself. Sweet baby Jesus…

—*Looks like we hit the jackpot.*—

Not until we can actually see our skin. She cringed, catching sight of her reflection in one of the heavy gilt mirrors hanging over the double sinks. And unfortunately, the sunken tub with jets running in the far corner wasn't gonna cut it. Kit sighed longingly at the mounds of bubbles, but this filth needed to go first.

Darke chuffed at her and jerked his head at the opening in the wall of square blocks of smoky glass beside it. Must be the shower. Poor cat. He needed to clean up, too. Kit went to turn on the water for him, thanking the Lord he wasn't even trying to groom that shit off himself.

It would be a tight squeeze, but she could probably help sluice off whatever he couldn't manage once she settled Cecelia. Kit eased the tiny dog out of her pocket, setting Grim's ruined cut and jacket aside, then filled up a sink and laid the tiny dog on a fluffy hand towel. That weird feeling she'd had gotten from the vamp fluttered in her chest. Had Hillary been looking for the little Pom?

—*Better question would be why.*—

Kit unfastened Cecelia's rhinestone collar and chucked it into the sink, her brow furrowing. *She probably wanted to do something horrible to her to upset Mr. Asorav. What did he say back at his flat?*

—*Girl, not for nothin', but he called the fucking thing his heart…*—

Kit's eyes went wide at the pathetic lump lying in a heap on the vanity. Holy shit, he had called the dog his heart. Did that mean—

She snorted out a laugh. *Nope. Not buying it. Damned dog eats its own shit and pisses in slippers. Besides, how stupid would that be? Frickin' thing tries to run into traffic every chance it gets.*

Kit's eyes pricked with tears, wondering if Cecelia would get any more of those. Shit. *Please don't die, please don't die…* She washed the poor thing off as best she could. Found a hairdryer and used it on the comatose Pomeranian, sniffling, re-donned its collar, then wrapped the dog in another hand towel, not knowing what to do.

—*Go shower, Kit. Take care of yourself.*—

She wiped her eyes, grit smearing her trembling fingers. Yeah. One thing at a time, right?

First things first, she needed to peel herself out of her disgusting clothes.

It wasn't easy. The filth from the pool had hardened stiff, and the material was stuck to her. Kit winced as everything came off, including some skin. She eyed the shower billowing steam and fingered the ring on her necklace. Damn. Darke was still in there…

Is it weird I don't want him to see me naked?

—*Are you for real right now?*—

She stopped at the entrance, biting her lip.

—*Girl, get in the fucking*—

A tattooed hand snaked out and grabbed her.

CHAPTER FOUR

GRIM'S mouth crashed down over Kit's, hands cupping her jaw, swallowing her scream. Goddamn, it'd been too long since he felt her. She struggled for a second and then gasped, pushing him beneath the spray.

"I thought—"

He silenced her with another kiss. Christ, he'd missed how she tasted, her scent… his cock kicked, and he pressed it against her belly, biting back a low moan. *Tell her cat about our game. We have to keep quiet. I don't care what that vamp said.*

[SULKING]

—Kat's mad—

Kat'll get over—Kit's hand cracked across his cheek, snapping his head to the side. Fuck! She glared at him, her bottom lip trembling, and the hurt in her eyes gutted him.

"I'm sorry," he mouthed.

She shot him double birds.

He held out his arms, and she looked like she was gonna hit him again, until her eyes fell on the pale circle of puckered scar the wight's bite had left. Her face screwed up, and she crumbled. Grim caught her as she fell, gathering her into his lap and holding her as her shoulders hitched with sobs. Goddamn it, this was not what… He sighed, moving her under the water and running his fingers through her matted hair. She shoved him away, doing it herself.

—says you're an asshole—

Yeah, I got that.

—Kat says me too—

Grim's head fell back against the shower wall, throat bobbing. Pissed there wasn't a fucking thing he could do to fix this shit show they were currently engaged in. He winced at the angry static biting at his consciousness, sure Kit's cat was giving his an earful.

Kit stood and grabbed a scrubby, attacking the filth on her. He tented his knees, head hanging, watching globs of shit get caught in the drain.

"I am so fucking mad," she hissed after an eternity of enraged silence, whipping a bottle of shampoo at him. Grim took the hit, his jaw clenching and knuckles going white with frustration.

Tell her—

—not listening—

You or her cat?

—both. bad game—

Jesus Fuck. Enough of this shit. Grim stood, grabbing Kit's wrists and pinning her against the tiles. *Tell her I get it, but we don't have time for this. It's safer for her if they think I'm not in the picture.* Her soapy chest heaved against his, bubbles trailing down her cheek. By the anger in those brown eyes, she wanted to beat the fuck out of him... and goddamn if it wasn't hot as hell.

Her rage softened as the buzz of their cats talking went back and forth, fading into the fall of water over smoky glass. He skated his fingers down her raised arm, trailing goosebumps. Kit's hips canted against his thigh with a needy sigh, an answering rumble built in his throat, her nipples hardening. The scent of her arousal perfumed the steamy air, and Grim's nostrils flared. He wet his lips, her heated gaze tracking the path of his tongue.

—Kat says she hates you—

Tell Kat she's a liar.

Kit gave a dismissive sniff, and pushed him away, rinsing herself off with the slow slide of her hands over her body. Her gaze flicked to his erection as he cupped it, a sly smile quirking up the corners of her mouth.

God fucking damn.

His hands caged her hips, cock rigid, smoothing against the slick skin of her abdomen, lips traveling up the column of her throat. The way he needed this woman... He rested his forehead against hers, breath heavy, desperate for her to see everything he felt in his eyes, how fucking sorry he was...

Her brow rose, thighs parting in invitation.

—says to apologize—

Grim smiled, kissing her softly, then dropped to his knees, burying his nose in her curls and breathing her in as she lifted a leg over his shoulder. He kissed the inside of her calf, the dimple of her knee... *Tell her I'm sorry. So fucking sorry...* His tongue ran the length of her honey-sweet slit, delving. Fuck, he loved her taste, her smell...

Kit's fingers knotted in his hair with a mewling cry, hips rocking. He parted her folds, exposing her creamy center and bit back a moan, lapping at it, thumb circling her clit, his cock aching. Her thighs trembled as one finger, then another slid between them, teasing, then scissoring deep. Jesus fuck, she was responsive. Slick velvet tightened around him, and Kit fisted his hair, breath speeding—

Her back arched with a low moan and a burst of sweetness glossed his lips, her cunt milking his fingers. Grim brought her down gently, slowing his motions until her last shiver had passed, his tongue laving her clean. She pressed back, sated and languorous against the cool tiles, the shower's steam blurring her expression of contentment as he lowered her leg to the floor.

Goddamn, she was fucking beautiful.

—claim her— his cat growled.

Grim's cock kicked at the thought, aching like a motherfucker, but he sat back on his heels, dashing water over his face. *This was an apology, not about me getting off.* He ran a hand down his throbbing length. *And trust me, I will, the second she says she wants it.*

Jesus, he wanted her to want it.

"I do..."

Grim's eyes snapped to Kit's. Did she just—

She bit her lip and gave a little nod, watching him stroke himself.

Pre-cum coated his hand, and he swallowed the lump in his throat. Fuck. Did she really want...

—CLAIM HER—

It's her first fucking time outside of a vibrator, asshole. The shower's not exactly where I envisioned doing this...

—lies—

Okay, fine, but in fairness, he'd imagined it pretty much everywhere—

"I said, I want it..." Kit's knees bracketed his hips, lowering herself down. "So fucking bad, Pussycat... show me what a real cock feels like," she whispered, one arm looping around his neck. "I'm ready..." Her hand circled his dick, dragging his crown through her slick folds.

Grim's eyes locked on hers, pupils dilating to swallow the warm brown of her irises as she notched him at her entrance. Her lips parted, brows knitting, working herself onto his thick length.

Jesus Christ—Grim groaned at the feel of her hot flesh slowly enveloping him. He gripped her hips, assisting her descent, heat shooting up his spine.

Fuck. Wasn't gonna last...

—no barbing—

Grim froze. *What? No. I told you—* He blinked, the comment tearing him from the brink. *Wait, you were the one who wanted—*

[FRUSTRATION]

—Kat says not yet.—

Well, then, if Kat says no—The tip of his cock burrowed deeper into her, and Kit threw her head back with a soft cry, offering up her glistening tits. *You know what? Do me a favor and fuck off for a while.*

Grim latched onto a peaked nipple, sucking the pebbled tip into his mouth. She rose up with a gasp, then down again, working her tight cunt onto his shaft. His fingers dug into her cheeks, kneading her ass, fighting his burning desire to spear into her wet heat.

Goddamn, she felt amazing wrapped around his dick...

"Jesus, baby. You take my cock so fucking good," he murmured, not giving a fuck if anyone could hear them anymore. She gasped again at the twitch of his hips driving him deeper, making her his. "Take it all, Kitten. Let me feed that greedy pussy."

Her arms wrapped around his neck, fingers tangling in his hair, and he devoured her mouth, tongues dueling, swallowing her cry as he thrust to the hilt, bottoming out. He groaned, Jesus fuck, this was fucking heaven. She was fucking heaven. His goddamned angel. Her walls tightened around him, a slick satin vise.

"Oh God... Grim..."

"Mmm... that's it, baby," he murmured against her lips. "Now move with me."

He kissed across her jaw and down her throat, nipping and sucking, his cock sliding counterpoint to the tentative rock of her hips. Goddamn, her inexperience turned him the fuck on, and she was all fucking his. Only his.

"You're mine." He thrust harder, his thumb dropping to strum across her clit, lips at her ear. "You like that? My hard dick inside you?"

"Oh God, yes..." Her movement smoothed out, getting

used to him, drawing farther up his shaft before slicking back down. "More… please…"

Approval rumbled through his chest, teeth teasing her earlobe. "Greedy girl. Begging so soon after taking my bare cock inside your sweet virgin pussy. You want more?" He slapped her clit, and she moaned, honey dripping down his sac, her walls trembling and so goddamned wet. "I'll give you fucking everything. You're mine, Kitten. Mine. Say it."

"I'm yours," Kit panted, her eyes rolling heavenward and breath stuttering.

"That's it, come all over my cock…" Jesus fuck—

Her cunt spasmed, pulling him in deeper and sucking at him, her pleasure a deluge, demanding his release. His balls drew up at the flood of her desire soaking over him, electricity zinging through his spine, light bursting through his skull. Hot ropes of cum painted the entrance to her womb, and he growled, wanting to pierce that divide, to plant his seed in her belly—

—Kat says no—

Grim laughed, flicking water from his eyes. He grinned at Kit's knitted brow. "Your cat says I can't knock you up yet."

Her cheeks pinked, and he kissed her softly.

"But I'm gonna. Soon, Kitten. Maybe not the next time I cream this pretty pussy until it drips down your thighs, but fucking soon." He traced a circle where her neck met her shoulder. "And when I do, my bite's gonna go right here. Mmm." He shifted his hips, hard again at the thought.

"What's stopping you from biting me now?" she asked, a little triangle of worry between her brows.

Grim brushed his fingers over it, then smoothed the lines away with a kiss. "The venom in a shifter's bite is really toxic to humans. I'm not gonna chance it until you turn."

Kit bit her lip, tracing the tattoos on his forearm to the gnarly scar the wight had left. "This was supposed to kill you?" He nodded, and she grabbed the soggy dick scarf from the shower floor. "You think I'm really the shifter queen, or was it this?"

"I dunno," he shrugged. "But you're my queen either way, whether you change or not."

"Pretty sure I will now."

"We gotta wait and see, baby, but I'm not opposed to slicing a vein to guarantee it."

"Can you do it later?" Brick said from outside the shower. "I mean, that session was hot as fuck, but I'd really like to rinse off."

—growling—

Kit paled, then went bright red, pushing Grim away and attempting to cover herself.

"Dude!" Grim growled over his shoulder. He stood, helping her to her feet and steadying her as she wobbled. "You okay?"

Kit nodded, running a hand over her flushed cheeks. "Yeah, just a little light-headed."

[WORRY]

Grim grunted, not sure he entirely believed her, and stuck his head out of the stall. Brick was in the tub, arms to either side, ruddy bubbles swirling around his pecs. He better not be jacking off in there. Fucker was getting on his last nerve. "Asshole."

"I told him to stay the fuck out," Deuce called from the other room.

—kill him—

Trust me, it's a possibility if he keeps this shit up. Grim grabbed a towel and passed it to Kit before wrapping another around his waist. "Then you get first dibs on the shower," he yelled back at Deuce.

"The fuck? I'm gettin' all pruny," the enforcer bitched, eye-fucking Kit as she stepped out of the stall, beet red and wrapped in a towel. His lips pursed, and he raised an eyebrow, head canted. "Damn, babydoll..."

—MINE!—

"Don't," Grim warned, pushing his cat back down and stabbing a finger at Brick.

He psh'd and leaned back, closing his eyes. "Whatev."

Grim stared at him for a second longer, his cat scrabbling to get out and drown the motherfucker. Grim couldn't blame him. Brick was just asking for a beatdown. He'd always been a dick, but ever since Clay had died, the enforcer seemed to get off on pushing Grim's buttons. Shit usually didn't faze him, but the fuck if he'd let Brick disrespect his mate.

Kit wrung out the scarf in the sink, then snagged Asorav's not-quite-dead dog from the vanity and hurried into the other room. She stumbled, cheeks flaring as she passed Deuce.

He paused to fist bump Grim, grinning ear to ear. "Nice to have you back, brother, and it's about fucking time you got your dick screwed on straight. Man needs a good woman, and that one's a fucking keeper. She's kept her shit together better than I'd expected."

Grim shook off his irritation with Brick, watching Kit lay the pathetic little mutt on the bed, draping the damp scarf over it. She ran a hand down her face again, frowning at the russet, Brick-sized stain in the middle of the bedspread, and the goddamned arsenal he'd disassembled and laid out like a buffet to dry.

Kit turned away, stumbling. Damn, beneath the flush of her cheeks, her skin was pale. Was she really okay? Before he could ask, she disappeared into the closet.

—something's wrong—

Wrong how?

—…—

That doesn't help. "Yeah, Kit's stronger than she looks." Grim scratched at his stubble, weirdly proud about that and wondering yet again what the fuck his cat was talking about. "You thinkin' about finally—"

"Fuck no," Deuce glared, a certain pigtailed-handful

remaining unmentioned. Grim backed toward the closet, hands raised. Sooner or later the stubborn fuck would admit he had it bad as for Triss as she did for him, but today was apparently not that—

Goddamn.

Grim froze in the closet's doorway. It was bigger than his room back at the club; the walls lined with clothes and some kind of tiered shoe-shrine was under a fucking spotlight in the middle of the space.

And the way Kit was stroking a green dress beside it made his cock jealous.

"You like that one?" he asked, stepping in. Christ, it had more shit to choose from than a superstore, and ain't none of it was from a clearance rack.

She turned with a laugh as he came in; her eyes too bright. "Like? It's frickin' Versace from this year's collection... and those," she pointed at a pair of strappy heels, "are custom Jimmy Choos..." Kit put a hand to her heart. "Like? No. I've died and gone to frickin' heaven. Oh, my—" Her free hand fluttered against her throat and she swayed. He reached out to steady her, and she batted him away. "Are those—"

She ran to a shelf and pulled out a pair of jeans, squealing, her feet beating a rapid tattoo against the floor. "Vintage Balenciaga," she said, like that explained everything.

Grim riffled his hair. "Uh, cool?"

She rolled her eyes at him. "Do not tell me you don't—No. You know what? Don't. When I tell Chanté—" Her brow crumpled and she teared up.

Fuck. He'd forgotten her best friend had been in that club explosion. Grim pulled her into his arms. Did she feel too warm, or was that from the shower?

—something's wrong—

"She's probably fine, Kit. Christ, Chanté's mom is the fucking witch queen. You think she'd let anything happen to her? I'm sure your bestie got out of the club fine." At least, he was pretty sure. Maybe. Sama was a serious cunt, but blowing up her own kid was next level. "You sure you feel all right?"

"You think so?" Kit sniffled, ignoring his concern.

"Yeah. She's probably just lying low. Didn't seem like you two were real keen on letting anyone know you were friends."

"No…" Kit smoothed a hand over the jeans, frowning. "I texted her when I saw her, and she said to play it that way. Her family… they're not real accepting of her lifestyle, or anyone in it. I-I think she was protecting me."

"She protected us both." Grim was positive that Chanté stepping in to perform that spell had saved his ass. "It hasn't even been twenty-four hours. Give it time. She'll reach out."

Kit took a deep breath and nodded, a sheen of sweat glistening over her brow.

[WORRY]

"Baby, you sure you're all right?"

"Yeah, yes, it's just… it's just been a lot, you know?" She eyed the room the way Brick had eyed her earlier. "Go see your boys. Imma need a minute—"

—stay—

We'll be right in the next room. Grim pulled her tight against him, stupidly jealous of fucking clothes. She gasped as he nipped at her jaw, "You better not be getting off on this shit. Your pleasure's mine, baby."

She laughed. "Yeah? And what you gonna do if I tell you Louis Vuitton will always be my first love?"

"Put a bullet in him."

Her laugh brought a broad grin to his face. "You're a century plus too late for that, Pussycat." She laughed again, flicking her fingers at the door. "Unless you're picking something out to dress that fine ass in, get outta here and let me find some clothes."

"Wear something you can run in, I gotta feeling we're not

in the clear yet," he murmured, kissing her fiercely and leaving her to it.

KIT FROWNED as Grim stalked out the door, eyeing those Choos. Unfortunately, he was probably right, as much as she wanted to wear that Versace, it would be a damned crime to fuck it up. She sighed, fingering the jeans she was holding. Not that ruining these would be much better, but nothing in here rated blue-light special status—

Her vision doubled again, and she put a hand to the wall, steadying herself. Despite what she'd told Grim, she really wasn't feeling well, but they had enough problems without adding hers into the mix. If she could nail HDL's year end close with the flu, she sure as hell could handle whatever this —Cold sweat swept over her body. *Ugh... what the hell is this?*

—*Another step in the change.*— Kat's voice held a smug tightness Kit wasn't sure she liked. —*We just gotta ride it out...* —

Easy for you to say. She winced, eyes closing at the wave of nausea churning through her gut. She panted, swallowing against her rising bile. *Wait, what do you mean, another*—

The constant low static in the back of her mind exploded into a hurricane of angry bees. Kit crumpled to the floor under the assault, taking down a rack of blouses with her. She gripped her temples, head feeling like it was gonna crack open. Grim called her name, and footsteps pounded in from the other room. Another wave of nausea swept over her and then—

Blackness.

RHYTHMIC THUMPING BEAT BACK at it. She whimpered, and strong arms pressed her closer against a massively muscled chest, the feel of it all wrong. Kit tensed, her heart rate spiking.

"I swear I'm not feeling you up," Brick's gravelly voice murmured against her hair, totally feeling her up.

Her eyes snapped open, and she pushed away from him. Ugh. "Where…?"

"Helicopter, headed north," he said as she took in the velour tracksuit and the tight-ass bandage tee she was wearing. Seriously, all that fashion porn and they'd put her in a fucking tracksuit?

Kit closed her eyes, biting back a scream. Nope, not gonna think about the jeans or that cashmere sweater she was gonna grab. Focus on something else. Like the helicopter—No, make that the damned air limo. Eight leather captain's chairs lined the oblong space of polished wood and bright metal. LED swirls in the ceiling softly lit Brick's smirk and picked up the red highlights in Deuce's dark hair.

He was grimacing in the chair to the right of them, one hand planted firmly over his stomach and the other white-knuckling the arm rest. Darke was stretched out at their feet, looking just as miserable, his claws buried in the dark gray carpeting, tail swishing, glowering at Brick with his ears flat against his head.

On the far side of the cabin, two vamps sat across from them.

One was Hillary, and the other… Yeah. Kit had zero doubt that the voluptuous redhead draped in jewels over houndstooth Burberry was Aryanna, the vampire queen. She didn't have any questions as to why she was sensitive about her appearance, either.

White-tipped fox ears peeked out of her tamed curls, and there was a pointed snout where her nose should be, her thin lips drawn up beneath it.

Kit swallowed, trying not to stare, but the queen's chill green eyes snared hers with the intensity of a predator's as she absently tatted lace, the light glinting off sharp, manicured claws.

"Did you enjoy your nap?" she drawled, her fingers moving like a completely independent creature. Damn, that was creepy, and not just the lace making and her fucked up features. Beneath them, Aryanna didn't look any older than Kit. The clothes and the crafting were just bizarre against her youthful frame.

Kit swallowed, dropping her gaze as she slid off Brick's lap into the empty seat to his left. Her vision wavered, and she took a slow breath, waiting for some stupid affirmation from her cat or a dig about not looking weak…

Crickets, and Kit had a really bad feeling Kat wasn't just avoiding her.

What the hell had happened? The change was supposed to let her beast out, not muzzle it… Aryanna's eyes tracked the bob of Kit's throat as she swallowed the gooey lump of "what the fuck is going on?" choking her up. Later. She'd figure it out later. Right now, not looking weak was a solid plan.

Yeah, just do that. Channel some bad ass bitch… except Kat was hers, and she'd apparently left the fucking building. Kit bit back a burble of manic laughter.

Okay, okay… She took a deep breath. Her cat would tell her to pull her ass together. Fake it till she made it… Kit crossed her legs and flicked her hair over her shoulder, smiling at the vamp queen like she was at a forensic accounting meeting and knew her client was guilty as fuck.

"You must be Aryanna, It's so nice to—"

"Don't insult me with empty pleasantries. I've neither the time nor the stomach for them. Being in such close proximity to your ilk is enough to test the latter," Aryanna said, her fingers speeding up while her attention stayed squarely on Kit. Beside her, Hillary smirked.

Okay, so that was how this was gonna go. Game on, bitch. Kit sat back and crossed her arms over her breasts.

The queen continued to glare at her. "Make no mistake, you are here for one reason and one reason only; payment of my unfortunate debt to Claymore James precludes me from expunging you. However, should that promise cost me my darkling…" Her green eyes frosted to jade, and the temperature in the cabin dropped. "You will see no more tomorrows."

[ANGER]

Kat? Silence and a weird pressure filled Kit's head. She shook it off, abruptly pissed as hell. If she wasn't in danger of this foxy bitch tearing out her throat, she sure as fuck wasn't gonna deal with her shitty attitude. "Noted. Meantime, seems like you having to lick Sama's ass is a bigger problem than me and my 'ilk.'"

Brick snorted back a laugh and man-spread in his chair, getting comfortable for the show. Beside him, Deuce started praying.

Hillary hissed, and the queen frowned, holding up a bejeweled hand. "Though crudely put, you're not wrong. You and I need to come to an understanding."

Kit cocked a brow, positive she wasn't gonna be down with whatever that meant.

"Sama is indeed an issue. Her unsanctioned culling of my people at the moot was beyond the pale, and sending a triad of Blēda to confront my darkling?" Her thin lips pressed together beneath her snout.

How the hell had she gotten like that? Something told Kit asking would be a bad thing. She fought not to look at Brick. *Oh God, please let him keep his fucking mouth shut…*

"I find the current situation most displeasing," Aryanna finished.

Kit resisted the urge to squirm in her seat at the icy chill emanating from the vamp queen. *Note to self, "most displeasing" equals super fucking pissed.* And no way was she gonna disagree that the witch queen had to go. If Aryanna could figure out how to make that happen, more power to her, but Kit wanted details on exactly what the current situation entailed.

"Hillary said they've taken Mr. Asorav to the Spire."

"Mmm. Did she now?" The queen's lips pinched down again, and Hillary looked nervous as fuck.

Huh. Wasn't that interesting. "She did. Is it true they can't de-animate him without his heart?" Kit asked, not so innocently before her stomach dropped. Shit. Cecelia. What had happened to the little dog?

Hillary's throat bobbed. Yep. Very fucking interesting. Brick pulled out his knife and started flicking it opened and shut, off beat to whatever he was softly whistling. God, she hated it when he did that.

"My, you had a much more enlightening chat than I was led to believe," the queen said with a tight smile, ignoring the big man. She paused her tatting, tapping the wickedly sharp tip of the oblong silver shuttle against her lips. "Let me be very clear; that bit of intel will not leave this cabin." She moved faster than Kit could track, and a crimson stain bloomed over Hillary's breast. "Nor will Ms. Birch."

"Nice," Brick murmured, pausing his whistling to adjust the bulge in his jeans.

Deuce smacked him. "Dude!"

[SATISFACTION]

Kat?

— … —

Hillary's eyes went wide, then grayed over, sinking into their sockets as they shriveled. Her flesh slackened, dripping from her cheekbones like melting wax, skin thinning to tear away from her features. Liquifying muscle and long strands of white tendon slipped from her skull, spattering onto her pantsuit.

Kit slapped a hand over her mouth. Holy Jesus fuck.

The queen adjusted her grip on the blood-stained shuttle and continued tatting, ignoring the corpse rapidly decomposing beside her. "But, seeing how my erstwhile companion has begun your education, I feel compelled to complete it."

A chunk of Hillary's scalp landed on the queen's armrest, and she flicked it away. "My darkling originated during a time when our sect was ascendant. His maker held several witches in thrall and had them devise a way of keeping him and his children safe during the daylight hours."

"By removing their hearts?"

"Just so. A spell was performed, and day-walkers were born. Staking, sunlight, silver—though not particularly pleasant, none of it de-animated them. As you can imagine, that caused quite a fervor."

Hillary's jawbone swung to one side, then thumped onto her lap. "Yeah, I'll bet," Kit swallowed, the off-key tune Brick was whistling making her insane. He started on the refrain for the umpteenth time. Why the hell did it sound famil—

Oh God. It was "Foxy Lady."

"The witches were dispatched almost immediately," the vampire queen continued, oblivious. Jesus fucking Christ, Kit hoped she was oblivious... She kicked Brick to knock it the fuck off, and his pursed lips smirked around the sour notes. "Of the five day-walkers that were made, two met their ends rather quickly as well. The third disappeared. The fourth was my mother."

"Was?" Kit jumped as Hillary's skull bounced onto the floor. It cracked like an egg, disintegrating into dust.

Brick kept whistling.

"Yes. Claymore James found her heart, and I took great pleasure in staking it." Aryanna lifted the shuttle to her lips and licked off a bit of gore. "A true queen is both born and made, Ms. Parson. Our bloodlines trace back to the first of our kind, allowing us to act as the wellspring of our sects' powers, but it also binds us. As long as our progenitors walk this earth, they hold sway over our actions."

Progenitors. Kit tensed, her mouth abruptly dry, and the asshole beside her started whistling a different tune. "Wait, are you saying—"

"Should you complete your transformation and become queen of the shifters, manifesting powers not seen for nigh a century, your father, Reaper Ells, will still be able to use his alpha command to make you do whatever his twisted, black heart desires. Which,"—she paused to inspect her lacework—"aside from his personal vendetta against Mr. James' biker club, is right in line with Sama's vision for the paranormal community."

Jesus. Kit wiped her palms against her thighs. She eyed Brick, trying to place a different damned refrain… "And what would that be?"

"Subjugation and the eventual eradication of the human population in the tri-state area to start. You know, something like they did to the fae way back when, tit for tat and all that," she said offhandedly. "Sama sees the shifters as boots on the ground for her incursion. Mr. Ells fancies himself general material and you his weapon. Their plan isn't totally without merit, but it would put my sect at a severe disadvantage. Aside from our thralls tasting so much better when they free range, our daytime logistics would be severely impacted should they succeed… Unless things were augmented by magic…"

"Deepening your debt to the witches."

Aryanna smiled unpleasantly at her. "Funny how that works out, isn't it?"

"I still don't understand what that has to do with Grim. The oculus—"

"Was the lesser of two evils devised to bring about the same result," she gave Kit a pitying moue. "I know for a fact the witch they'd slated to administer the spell had orders to make sure Mr. James didn't survive it... The question is, why did another of Sama's brood take her place?"

"I dunno," Kit deadpanned. No way was she spilling about Chanté. "Did the rest of our crew get out of the city?"

Aryanna pursed her lips as she unwound a length of spider-silk fine thread from her skein and wrapped it around her clawed fingers. "Let's try that again, Ms. Parson. Your mouth may lie to me, but your pulse does not. And your 'crew' is traveling north as we speak, though somewhat less luxuriously, I'm afraid."

"Thank you for that." Kit fought to keep a straight face as she finally recognized Brick's tone-deaf rendition of "20th Century Fox." Did he have a goddamned death wish? "And not for nothin', but my biology's been a bit off lately."

"Touché." Aryanna's eyes flicked to hers, then dropped to her tatting. "In either event, the witch in question was also brought to the Spire, which leads me to believe that there is a great deal more dissent in Sama's ranks than previously believed. And if it extends under her own roof, then the recent rumors of them losing one of the more powerful artifacts in their possession gains a considerable amount of traction—As do my plans for grinding her into dust." She looked over at Hillary's remains and smiled.

"An artifact?" Kit asked, mentally willing her pulse to calm the fuck down and her eyes to stay dry at the news Chanté was alive. Ironically, Brick being an asshole helped.

"Yes. A construct of power made in response to the day-walker's creation. Sama has been diligently gathering the few that've survived the ages. Most of the remaining artifacts are of no never mind, like the one my darkling shielded his inner rooms with, but the cloche was instrumental in her sect's ascension. If the rumors of its loss are true, she's never been more vulnerable, and with your arrival on the scene…" Aryanna's smirk went smug. "Well, I'd say the universe is sending a very clear message that it's time for a regime change." Her expression didn't leave any doubt as to who she thought was gonna come out on top if that happened.

Kit fought not to roll her eyes. Like for real, who had the fucking time or energy for this shit? All she wanted was a bottle, some tacos, and to Netflix and chill. Rich people had issues, but whatever. She could play along. "All right, I'm with you so far, but it still doesn't explain why Sama's going after Grim."

The vamp queen sighed, wadding up her lace and setting it aside. A film clouded her eyes, turning them a steely jade, and the air thickened. Deuce went still, and Brick's knife froze mid-snick, his whistling cutting off like someone had unplugged his mic.

Thank fucking God.

Darke growled, eyes narrowing at Aryanna, and his lip pulling up over his canines.

"Well, that's unexpected." The vamp queen's gaze swept over him and landed on the patch of white fur where the wight had bitten him. Her eyebrow rose. "You're much further along in your transition than I'd surmised…"

"What did you do to them?" Kit asked, not liking how Aryanna was looking at her.

"No lasting harm. It's vital that what I'm about to say only leaves your lips to pass into your heir's ears. Do you swear it will be so?"

"Um…" Kit fiddled with her sleeve, not entirely sure that was a great idea, but… "Yes?"

The queen's lips pursed beneath her snout. "Mr. James' existence is problematic for several reasons. The first of which is that he's actively transitioning you to queen, which Sama had hoped to avoid. That he's also your fated mate makes that infinitely worse."

Darke put his head against Kit's leg, and she reached down to stroke between his ears. "Why?"

"Because everything I told you about a progenitor's hold over us is true... unless you've been bred by your fated mate. Should that happen, and you slip Reaper Ells' leash, Sama's only recourse is to apprehend Mr. James and use his wellbeing to guarantee your compliance."

"Which is why she's framing him for the explosion..." Kit chewed her lip. "So you're saying once I'm knocked up, Reaper's alpha command won't work on me?"

"Correct. At that point, our bloodline's onus falls to the child, and we are free."

Kit sat, blinking. "But they won't be..."

A flicker of sadness passed over the vampire queen's face. "No," she said softly. "They are not... unless said progenitor no longer walks the earth, and make no mistake, someday, your child will look at you the same way you look at Reaper Ells. There is a price for power, Ms. Parson, and that is ours."

"I don't believe you," she whispered.

"Do or don't," the vampire queen shrugged. "That won't change the facts. Including that there's a cell beside the one my darkling's in, waiting for the beast at your feet, and I sincerely doubt he's as resilient." Kit was silent, and Aryanna smirked, releasing the others from her enchantment. Brick's suicidal whistling filling the cabin as she looped her thread around her fingers and began tatting again in earnest.

"There's a phone for you in that jacket." The queen motioned to the crumpled pantsuit on the seat beside her. "Should you find yourself in dire straits, there's a contact listed as 'Takeout.' Use it."

Kit stood and approached the wad of clothes. Nothing remained of Hillary, not even a bloodstain on the jacket's breast. Kit picked it up, fingering the oblong hole.

The vampire queen tsk'd. "I suppose that won't be

making it into the guest room closet with my other memorabilia. Pity. It was such a smart cut on the right frame."

Hold the fuck up... memorabilia? Kit swallowed, looking down at her tracksuit and feeling sick. Her mind flicked to the serial killer shows Chanté was obsessed with. Were all those clothes from people the queen had murdered?

"Waste not, want not, Ms. Parson." Aryanna murmured over her lace like she knew what Kit was thinking.

Kit dug out the latest i-whatever from the dead vamp's jacket, clenching its red rhinestone case on the way back to her seat in an effort not to freak the fuck out. Not even trying to figure out what Brick was whistling now helped. Kit swallowed. She was wearing something someone had been murdered in... Oh God...

—Calm down—

Kat?!

—Ugh. Stop yelling. My head feels like a party line.—

What the hell is a party line?

—A shit ton of people talking at the same time and none of them will shut the fuck up!—

Oh... Crap, the vamp queen hadn't stopped talking either.

"...took the liberty of having the information transferred over from your pervious device," she continued. "I can assure you, the coverage on this plan is much better than the one Ms. Sue procured for you."

Sweat prickled over Kit's scalp. Shit. The vamp queen knew about Chanté. Well, about her persona outside of the paranormal world, but it didn't sound like Aryanna had put together that Chanté Sue was also the witch that'd stepped up to do the oculus spell on Grim.

Not yet, at least. The queen was watching her again with that predatory glare. Kit busied herself with her new blinged-out phone. Damn. Rich people might have issues, but the perks sure were nice.

A golden light chimed on at the head of the cabin, and

Aryanna's eyes flicked from Kit to it in annoyance. "How unfortunate. We'll have to put a pin in that conversation, shall we? We're coming up on the drop point. Sergeant Arroyo—"

The behemoth broke off mid-bar, snapping his knife closed. "Name's Brick."

"As discussed, your van will be waiting for you," the vamp queen continued like he hadn't spoken. "I trust you can find your way home from there?"

He snorted, pocketing the blade. "Tarrytown ain't exactly off the beaten path."

"Splendid. I'll take that as a yes."

"Wait," Kit said, looking between them. "You're not taking us all the way to Flatts?"

"No. I've a presser scheduled with Sama." Aryanna's tone made it clear that was going to be anything but pleasurable. "She's no doubt eager to publicly cast aspersions upon my sect after my darkling eviscerated yet another one of her Blēda. You'd think she'd have learned better by now. Apparently, they're ever so difficult to replace." She smiled, pulling her tatting back out and smoothing the intricate lacework across her lap.

"Though injured, the other two will be out there. Once given a directive, a triad won't stop until its objective has been satisfied. I very much doubt my darkling was their target."

The helicopter descended, taking Kit's stomach with it. Deuce stood, jamming the straps of an over-stuffed Hermès tote over his shoulder. She swept her hand over the Etoop leather. "Are you for real?"

He shrugged. "Had to shove Grim's cut and all your stuff into something."

Huh? She didn't have any stuff... *Oh my God...* was Cecelia in there? The helicopter touched down, and Kit didn't have a chance to look. Brick scooped her up and the next thing she knew, he'd jumped out and was hunched low, running across a moon-lit field with her in his arms. Deuce and Grim followed, hot on his heels, to a black van waiting in the shadows. The helicopter was airborne before Brick got the driver's side door open. He shoved her inside, Deuce and Darke piling into the back.

"Ok, what was that last song?" she asked the enforcer, knowing she was gonna regret it.

"Oh, come on, you didn't recognize 'Fox on the Run?' That shit's classic." The sliding door slammed shut, and Brick laughed like a goddamned maniac, peeling out onto a country road and breaking into off-key song.

Kit scrabbled for the seatbelt. If they made it back alive, she was gonna frickin' kill him.

CHAPTER FIVE

GRIM SHIFTED BACK to two legs and snagged the bag of crap they'd liberated from the vamp queen's trophy closet. Until they were back in Flatts, it was a hell of a lot more likely someone would call in a mountain lion than a guy who might look like one of America's Most Wanted.

—'cause i'm better looking—

Grim snorted *Yeah, that's the reason.* He pulled on a pair of jeans and a tee before sticking his head between the front seats. Brick had picked up Route 9, heading north instead of cutting across the Hudson on 287. Shit was gonna take them way too deep into Westchester County, which was solidly witch territory. "Any reason we're headed this way?"

"S'a method to my madness, brutha, just sit your ass in the back and keep outta sight. You too, babydoll, and while you're at it, trade me that fancy phone." He pulled a rectangular Velcro pouch out of his inside jacket pocket and flipped it at her.

"My name's Kit, asshole." She looked at the pouch like it was communicable. "What is it?"

"I got it," Grim said, ripping the pouch open and dumping Brick's burner onto the center console. The phone the vamp queen had given Kit was a tight fucking fit, but he managed to squeeze it in and seal it up. "It's a Faraday phone sleeve. If they've got any sketchy tech on there, listening, tracking, whatever, that'll block it." Not that the entire van wasn't bugged, but it was one less thing to worry about until Mouse could take it apart back at the clubhouse.

Kit's brow quirked at Brick as she unbuckled and traded places with Deuce. "And you just happen to have one of those on you?"

"Right up my ass, next to the tent and the MREs," the enforcer grinned, speedometer pegging ninety on the narrow two-lane road. "Deuce, you wanna text in? I'd do it, but driving distracted's illegal," he said, blowing through a red light.

"Happy to, wouldn't want to break any laws." Deuce murmured absently, his thumbs already tapping at the screen.

"Are they always like this?" Kit asked, turning to Grim.

"Like what?"

She just looked at him, then shook her head.

—she means idiots—

Yeah, I got that. Grim riffled his hair. *Seriously buddy, go the fuck to sleep or hang out with Kat.*

—can't—

What do you mean you can't?

—she's busy—

"I can't believe you shoved your filthy jacket into a Hermès bag..." Kit sighed, carefully sifting through it to hand him his wallet and pull out the pathetic bundle of fur wrapped in her dick scarf. Dog was still out cold. "What do you think is wrong with her?"

"Dunno." Grim shrugged, not in the damned mood to play twenty questions with his cat. *Would it kill you to use complete fucking sentences?* He sat behind Kit so she could lean against his chest.

[FRUSTRATION]

Yeah, you and me both.

—dog's like Kat—

Kat's fucking comatose?

[AGITATION]

—no, she's busy—

"Maybe Cecelia hit her head?" Kit's brow furrowed, her fingers tracing the dog's skull. "I don't feel a bump or anything."

"Keep her wrapped up. We can take her to the vet's when we get into town. Triss's good with animals." Maybe she could figure out what the fuck his cat was talking about while she was at it.

[AGITATION]

—witches— his cat hissed, tail lashing, all riled up and frustrated as fuck.

Grim rubbed a temple, hating it when the asshole got like this. *What about them?*

—made you busy—

Okay, now they were getting somewhere. Grim sat up straighter. *Her and the dog are fucked up like that? In their minds?*

—no—

Jesus fucking—

"Think we got bigger issues than the vamp's poodle," Deuce called back from the front seat.

"Pomeranian," Kit corrected.

"I don't give a fuck if it's a piglet, Wrench and Doc ain't gettin' back to me."

"Isn't it past two in the morning?" Kit asked.

"Yeah, but Wrench don't sleep," Deuce muttered, pulling at his lip. "Not normal hours at least, and when he does, he's got a hair fucking trigger, and Doc's used to being on call. One of 'em taking a couple minutes to hit me back I can see, but nothing from both of them? Shit ain't right."

"Vamps could'a made 'em ditch their phones," Brick said after a minute.

Grim grunted, agreeing. He would've in their position. "Try MK."

—growling—

Both Deuce and Brick glanced back at him like he was crazy.

"Can't imagine you're his favorite person after all the shit his sweet baby girl's been spreading about you," Deuce said.

Kit frowned. "MK's Nikki's dad?"

"Yeah, and he's not at the top of my list either…" Shit, did he tell them his suspicions? Spilling to Stitch was one thing, but if he was wrong, Brick wouldn't fucking hesitate to use his goddamned blow torch to sear the club ink from Grim's back… but if he didn't and was right, they might not have a club at all. He scrubbed a hand over his face. Fuck it. "I think MK might be the rat."

The van swerved. "MK?" Brick asked, pulling back into their lane. Deuce turned to look at him, his brows furrowed.

"Yeah. When Nikki first started spreading shit about Kit being Reaper's daughter and all that crap about an alliance between me and him, MK knew it was bullshit and didn't say dick. He was the one who clued me into who Kit was when she showed up at the clubhouse. Said Clay had offered her sanctuary and explained everything in his will."

"Did he?" Deuce asked.

"I dunno, I never looked at the fucking thing, but—" Shit. Grim reached around Kit to the bag and grabbed his jacket, hoping the manilla envelope MK had slapped down on the bar was still in his pocket—

It was and nasty as fuck.

Kit winced. "Sorry, I didn't know where else to put Cecelia. It's not ruined, is it?"

"Envelope's toast, dunno about what's inside." Grim peeled the frayed, soggy brown paper back, not real hopeful. A key pinged onto the floorboards and Kit picked it up. Whatever it went to, it wasn't from this century. Grim handed the remaining two or three damp pages of cramped, single-spaced type up front for Deuce to figure it out.

"You're not gonna read it?" Kit asked.

He tensed. "No."

"But—"

"Asshole's dyslexic," Brick said, digging out his flashlight for Deuce and laughing at Grim's growl. "What? Like it's a fucking secret. Plenty of people are. My younger brother couldn't read if his life depended on it. You just take fucking forever."

"Thanks, shithead," Grim muttered, glowering out the windshield. Fuck, now Kit was gonna think he was stupid.

—not—

She snuggled back against him, cradling Asorav's dog, and Grim sighed. *No, we're not.*

They'd driven into a more populated area, and Brick slowed down, throwing on a blinker.

"Gotta piss," he said, meeting Grim's eyes in the rearview.

Right. More like he was gonna jack a car. Grim started shoving shit back into the bag. "Hold on to that," he said, folding Kit's fingers over the key. She nodded and took off the necklace he'd given her to thread it onto the chain.

Brick pulled into an apartment complex and killed the engine. "Gimme five," he said, getting out.

"I still can't believe MK's the rat," Deuce muttered, scanning the first page. "I mean, it tracks, but..."

"Deacon running a fucking prostitution ring under Clay's nose was pretty un-fucking-believable, too, but it still happened," Grim said, shrugging into his grimy inside-out cut and looping the bag over his shoulder. He grabbed Kit's hand. "Come on, if we're stopping, I'm taking the opportunity piss too."

Her eyebrow quirked. "You need me to hold it?"

"Yeah, baby." He grinned, kissing her. "Something like that."

"Ugh. I think I liked it better when you were a miserable fuck," Deuce muttered, getting out of the van, papers in hand.

"Get used to it." Grim slid open the side door. "Or better yet, maybe you should try it sometime."

"Fuck off. She's too young."

Kit looked between them as she stepped out of the van into the blistering wind, cradling Asorav's dog. She shivered, hunching her shoulders, and tucked the tiny mutt between her tits.

"What?" she asked at Grim's raised brow. "I don't want her to get cold."

"Lucky dog."

Kit rolled her eyes. "Who's too young?"

"Triss," Grim said at the same time Deuce muttered, "Nobody."

Deuce glared at him and Grim's grin widened.

"Triss? She's only a year or two younger than me, and you're Grim's age, aren't you?"

A shitty sedan crept up behind them. The dark-tinted driver's side window lowered and Brick jerked his head at them to get in.

"I'm older." Deuce grumbled, snagging shotgun.

Grim held the door as Kit slid in the back, flicking fast food wrappers from the seat. "Yeah, by a whopping sixteen months."

"I don't see the problem," she said, a look of pure disgust on her face as Grim climbed in beside her. He couldn't disagree. The ride Brick had jacked was a fucking dumpster on wheels.

"Deuce is the only one who does," the enforcer said, pulling out of the complex.

"Fuck all y'all. How about we stop discussing what's not gonna fucking happen and start talking about what is. What's the plan?"

"Keep driving north." Brick said, getting back on 9. "Wasn't gonna risk the cameras on the Tappan Zee. Figure we'll have better luck sneaking west on 6."

"Bear Mountain still has fucking tolls, dude." Which meant cameras. Grim scrubbed at his face. "And that route adds what, a couple of hours onto the trip?"

"There's no tolls on the bridge if you're heading west, and it'll add an hour forty-five, tops. Trust me, I can make that up. They'll expect us to go through Albany. This pile's got enough in the tank to make it to Binghamton. We'll swap it out there and head up 81."

"We will, huh?" Grim's teeth clenched at the asshole's decree.

"Sorry, I should have said 'we are.'" He met Grim's eyes in the review and no doubt about it, that motherfucker was challenging him. Fur rippled over Grim's knuckles.

—KILL!—

Deuce cleared his throat. "So, why do you wanna text MK if you think he's dirty?"

Grim sat back, jaw muscles popping. *Not the time or place. Don't worry. Fucker will get his...* "That's just it, I don't know he is, and I don't fucking know if the vamps were on the up and up about getting the rest of the crew home." Grim put an arm around Kit at her soft cry of protest. "You gonna keep that thing in there?" he asked, eyeing the two-pound lump of dog peeking out of her tight shirt.

"Jealous?"

"Very." Grim growled, catching Brick eye-fucking her in the rearview.

[RAGE]

Yeah. I get a go at the son of a bitch first.

—no hamstringing—

No promises. Grim frowned, turning back to Deuce. "Text MK some general bullshit feeling him out and see what he hits us back with."

"Sec... asking him what the fuck is going on up there..." Deuce tapped at the phone and a second later, it pinged. "Wants to know where we are and what the hell happened.

Nothing about the crew, but they're only like an hour or two ahead of us, tops. Doesn't sound like he knows shit."

"Stitch woulda found a way to call in by now…" Grim scratched at his stubble. "Give him the CliffsNotes about the explosion and the oculus fucking me up. With Deacon still in jail, and Stitch MIA, that leaves MK and Miser as the only ones up there with a seat at the table. Tell him we're stuck in the city, and that he's gotta postpone the vote."

"And if MK pushes it through without a fucking quorum, we'll know he's dirty, and you've got proof he knew what really went down before the vote…" Brick murmured. "Nice. You're smarter than you look."

Grim frowned at him. "Thanks, asshat."

"Oh, no. The pleasure is all mine."

Deuce let out a deep sigh and sent the message. This time, it took a lot longer to ping. "He says he'll see what he can do."

"The fuck? See what he can do?" Brick's knuckles tightened on the wheel.

"Pretty sure at this point, Grim's right, and *Robert's Rules of Order* do not apply," Deuce said, flipping the phone onto the dash and picking up Clay's will again.

"No, but they're gonna hurt like hell when I shove that fucking book up MK's ass," the enforcer growled, slowing as he navigated a rotary with gritted teeth. "I hate these goddamned things."

"You hate everything," Grim muttered, sitting back and putting his arm around Kit.

"You should talk," Deuce said, kicking taco wrappers away from his feet and settling back to read. "Am I the only one who's fucking starving all of a sudden?"

—no—

Go the fuck to sleep.

"Yes," everyone else in the car replied.

Kit scooted closer as the road got steeper and the tree line fell away, the full moon revealing an expansive view of the Hudson and a shit ton of jagged rocks on the way down to it. Brick kept following the road up the mountainside and around what wasn't quite a hairpin turn.

"So what does it say?" Kit asked Deuce, her fingers digging into Grim's thigh.

He took her hand in his and kissed her knuckles. "Heights bother you?"

"Eighty story building, no. This? Hell, yes."

Deuce sucked on his teeth. "From what I can make out, Clay's will pretty much says what MK told you it did. Names you his heir, gives you all his crap except for that piece of shit house we burned down. He left that and the property it's on to Kit… Your middle name is Augusta?" He and Brick looked at each other and snickered.

"It was my grandmother's name, asshole."

Grim kissed her temple. "It's a fucking fast-ass Italian bike, too."

"Spelt different," Brick snorted. "You and your Euro-trash relics. When the fuck you gonna ditch that shit and buy something this century American like a true patriot?"

"Dunno," Grim grumbled with a pang for his Bobber. He was gonna be fucking pissed if he never saw that bike again. "Maybe when they stop importing all their shit from Asia. Anything after nineteen—"

"Dude!" Brick yelled over Deuce's laughter. "I swear to Christ, you start spouting that shit, and I'll drive this pile off the fucking—"

The backend fishtailed, and Kit screamed, clutching onto Grim.

"Hey, stop fucking around!"

"Shit, I'm not, I think we blew a goddamned—"

The door next to Kit ripped open, and she was jerked out of the car, into the night.

CHAPTER SIX

DARKE BURST out of his man, both of them in agreement as he tore out of the car after Kit. She shrieked, a gray-robed figure manhandling her as they flew up the mountainside. Back at the car, Deuce and Brick yelled, and a shot rang out.

A pattering of dirt fell to Darke's left and an unyielding weight slammed into him, sending him tumbling back down to the road.

He twisted mid-air, his ribs screaming, and hit the gravel hard, skidding to face a second robed figure emerging from the shadows, clutching his bleeding arm. Darke's hackles rose, a growl in his throat, ready to spring.

The Blēda had found them, and one of those fuckers had his mate.

Brick fired again, and a sickly green light flared around the witch. He waggled a finger. "Fool me once, shame on you, fool me twice… well, that's not going to happen." He swept a hand in front of himself, and a flurry of scree sliced through the air, battering against them. Darke flattened himself to the ground beneath the barrage, ears back and snarling.

Deuce swore, diving behind the car, but Brick held his position, still firing. The yowls and hisses of their cats blathering filled the back of Darke's mind, the noise searing at his skull just shy of one of his man's migraines and setting his teeth on edge.

I think he's trying to draw the witch's attention while Deuce shifts, his man said. *Get on the prick's right side while he's distracted.*

Darke crouched low and sprinted to the other side of the road. Halfway there, the air pressure changed. He sprang to the side, just missing a massive boulder crashing down to cratering the asphalt where he'd been, his trajectory taking him up, over the guardrail—

Oh shit!

Darke yowled, twisting, legs splayed, searching for something, anything, to stop him from careening into the void below. A finger of stone broke off as he smashed into it, claws scrabbling for purchase on a scant ledge far below the road. He dangled, panting, hindquarters pinwheeling for purchase.

—*Fuck, did Darke go over?*—

He lost his grip at the unfamiliar voice in his mind, slipping. His claws dug in, tips shattering against the stone as he slowly drew his hindquarters up onto the spit of ledge. Sides heaving, he pressed himself against the cliffside.

—*Don't care. Gonna shift. Draw fire.*— Flashes of green light and another barrage of stones rained down from above. A lynx yowled, hit.

Darke! We gotta get back up there, his man yelled, frantic to get to their mate.

Darke's heart pounded, fairly certain he'd just used up at least one of his lives, but more freaked out that he could understand Brick and Deuce's cats. How was that possible?

—*Pretty sure it's a side benny to having a queen, Boy Vengeance.*—

His ears quirked forward. Kat. She wasn't busy anymore. —*Kit?*—

—*Imma take care of her, you need to take care of your boys.*—

His boys. Darke's eyes went wide. A Pride. He could have

a pride now. Not just Grim. Maybe. Talk. They'd want him to talk. Like Kat…

Darke! The fuck is up with you?! his man yelled. *Get off this fucking ledge and shred that asshole! We gotta get to Kit!*

Darke chuffed his agreement, inspecting the cliffside. He gathered his hindquarters beneath him and sprang to one outcropping and then another, working his way back up the mountain.

Light flared, the boom of a violent explosion resounding through the night. Stones crashed down, breaking off huge chunks of the cliffside as they fell, and shearing off Darke's means of escape. He flattened himself into a crevice, trapped, the squeal of stressed metal standing his fur on end.

Above, the car teetered over the abyss, front axle caught in the guardrail. It hitched, dipping lower, bolts tearing from the supports like the slow click of a minute hand.

The lynxes' yowls and hisses were frenzied, purely animalistic cries of rage.

Another support's bolts pinged into the night, and the car dropped lower.

You gotta jump.

Darke growled at his man's assessment, gauging the distance. His legs bunched with the long, slow shriek of straining metal—

He leaped as the next support gave, hitting the car's back window and twisting as he sprang off. The remaining bolts let go, firing like bullets, and a long snake of twisted steel whipped from the cliffside, following the car down into the Hudson.

Darke bounded off the ribbon of metal it as it fell, bolstering himself one last time to reach to the lip of the road…

His midsection hit the cliff's edge, driving the breath from him. Ahead, the lynxes had the witch backed against the mountain. All of them were beat to shit and bloodied, and at a stalemate.

Darke growled, clawing his way onto solid ground and stalked forward.

Deuce's lynx caught sight of him and almost fell over. —*The fuck?*—

—*not dead*— Darke sent back, his lips peeling away from his teeth.

But this fucker was about to be.

KIT SCREAMED, the wind whipping the sound away as it left her lips. Distantly, she heard a thunderous explosion and cats yowling. Whoever had her chuckled low in his throat, the sound reverberating through her with an icy sense of dread. She struggled against her captor as they swept up the mountainside, and a blade pressed against her throat.

"Don't," a cultured voice purred beside her ear. "I've orders to collect you, but aside from breathing, my mistress didn't specify what condition you needed to arrive in."

Kit went limp. Oh God, the Blēda... but how had they found her?

"Good girl," he crooned, landing on an outcropping of stone, his torn gray robe whipping about his legs. His features were hidden within the shadows of a deep hood, but the eyes staring out at her burned. "Shall we watch the show?"

The show? He jerked her head downward, back the way they'd come. The car was nowhere to be seen, and the road had been blown to shit, boulders and debris making it impassable. Grim and the others were in cat form, circling a second robed figure. Darke let out an ear-piercing yowl and lunged—

Kit sobbed, screwing her eyes closed. She couldn't look. *Oh my God, Oh my God...*

—Don't you worry, baby girl, Darke's tearing that motherfucker up, and I got you.—

Kat?

—You know it. Now sit back and let me deal with this sack of shit.—

Before she could ask Kat what she meant, her vision doubled and a horrible ripping sensation went through her. Kit screamed, dropping to her knees. The witch behind her laughed, intent on the action below, fisting a clump of her hair. Kit's fingers curved, tendons stretching and bones elongating. Her jawbone popped, teeth sharpening to points…

And stopped.

—Damn it, I can't get all the way out yet!—

Then go back in! Kit screamed at Kat, frantic.

—The hell I am, girl—

"Open your eyes and watch, bitch," the Blēda spat out, shaking her like a doll.

—Oh no he didn't…—

Kit's consciousness was pitched backwards as Kat streamed forward, taking over their body. She spun to her feet in one sinuous motion, claws slicing through the witch's robes and ripping into the soft meat of his belly, shredding his intestinal wall. Her teeth found his throat and clamped down, cutting off his shriek as she bit through his windpipe. He fell back, fighting to escape, and Kat yowled, riding him to the ground. His head hit the rocky terrain with a sickening crack, and the witch went still. Hot torrents of blood pulsed over Kat's chin, sticky and hot, slowly stuttering to a seeping trickle.

She pushed off him, spitting out a chunk of trachea and ran her sleeve over her mouth. Man tasted like shit. Flavor went with his attitude. "Bitches are dogs, asshole. I'm a fucking cat."

Someone behind her began slow clapping. "Indeed, you are."

Kat retreated, leaving Kit staggering to turn and face the voice. A middle-aged man in a formal kurta, like the one Chanté had been wearing at the moot, was sitting on a nearby outcropping of stone. She bit back a burble of manic laughter, so fucking done with all this shit. Vampires, witches, weird yogis on a mountain... Where the fuck was her calculator and some long form reconciliation sheets?

"Who the hell are you?" she asked, slumping against the cliffside before she fell over.

"Ah, forgive me, I'm remiss." The wind dropped off as he cleared his throat and stood, giving her an exacting bow. "Shamir Dhar, king witch to the uninitiated, perpetually displeased with—and displeasing to—my sect, and Chanté's father; at your service."

Kit's eyebrow rose. She could see the resemblance, but claiming to be Chanté's dad wasn't winning him any brownie points after the way Sama had treated Kit's bestie. Although... "*Chanté's* father?"

"Yes, and I must admit, my being here is in direct protest to her current plight. I'm afraid Sama and I don't see eye to eye when it comes to our parenting methods. She's a bit of a tiger mom, I'm more of a free-range dad... We really should've discussed our ideologies more before getting married, but, what can I say? I was put in a bit of a Meatloaf moment all 'what's it gonna be boy,' and, well, she had a great ass. In retrospect, I really should've slept on it."

Kit blinked at him. "Are you for real right now?"

"As far as I know..." Shamir patted his chest like he was checking. "Why, did I flicker?"

"N-no..."

"Oh, thank goodness. Spatial displacement can be a bit dicey..." He laughed, slapping his knee. "Woo! It'd be rather embarrassing if I came all this way to help you, only to find myself still in my study. Astral projections are all flash and no bang, if you know what I mean."

She nodded. Nope. Not a fucking clue.

—Man's batshit—

Kit pinched the bridge of her nose at the understatement. "So let me get this straight. You're the king fucking witch—"

"Ooh, I like that. The king *fucking* witch." He tapped his lip. "Adds a bit more gravitas, doesn't it?"

"—your wife just sicced a triad on me, but you wanna help because you're pissed she's got Chanté locked up in the Spire."

"Mmm. Yes. In a nutshell." He held out a long-fingered hand. "Shall we go down? I believe they've dispatched the poor sod below. Rather quickly, too, I might add. I told Rasheed and Harold their arrogance would be their demise, and as usual, I wasn't wrong."

Kit glanced at the mauled body on the ground. The wind had flicked back the Blēda's hood. Her stomach turned. He didn't look much older than her. She rubbed her fingers against her palms, gore pebbling up beneath nails that didn't seem capable of—

She swallowed her rising bile, head going light. Jesus Christ, she'd done that…

—No, we did that. Well, mostly me, but I guess you were there, too…—

A monster. She was a fucking monster. Kit slid to the ground and gripped her knees, the reality of what'd just gone down hitting her hard. Auntie Jojo, her mother, they'd been right…

Oh God, what have I done?

Kit's fingers curled against her temples, a ragged sob at her lips.

—Kit! No, it's not like that—

The fuck it wasn't. This. This right here. This was why she'd sworn she'd never become a shifter. She was turning into a fucking animal. She couldn't control it. Couldn't stop herself. Kat had ripped right through her, forced her back—

Sweet baby Jesus, was she feral? Is that what it felt like for Grim? To be shoved down into your mind and forced to watch a part of you do horrible things?

—I didn't—it wasn't—

Murder. She'd murdered that man. Tasted his blood on her tongue—

Her stomach revolted, and she vomited, a horrible mineral funk spattering at her feet.

Long-fingered hands held back her hair, and she broke down. Shamir sat beside her, rubbing her back as she totally lost her shit. When her ugly crying subsided, he handed her a bottle of water from God knew where. She sniffled, wiping the snot from her lip, almost seeing the kindly man Chanté had described.

Until he started talking again.

"You know, your first kill is always the easiest," he mused as she swished and spat.

Kit wiped her nose again, sniffling. "What?"

"It's true. Now you know how you're going to feel afterwards. Takes the fun out of it. Well, unless you're a psychopath, then I suppose that feeling *is* the fun. Ooh, that reminds me." He crawled over to the Blēda's corpse and riffled through its pockets.

Kit watched him pull out the dead dude's wallet, numb. "You're mugging him?"

"Hmm?" Shamir absently pocketed a wad of cash and kept flipping through the billfold. "Does it qualify as mugging if he's dead, or would that be grave robbing? I always get tripped up by the semantics in situations like these..." The was a slight scuff on stone and his head snapped up, a broad smile splitting his lips.

Darke sat in the shadows, tail curled around his feet, watching the witch. At his back prowled two lynxes, easily the size of German Shepards.

"Ah! Mr. James, right on time. Here. This is for you." He

stood, holding out a black key card. "I know you're in there," he cajoled, waggling the rectangle of plastic in front of the big cat. "Go on, take it. Take it. Taaake itt…"

Darke chuffed, and a moment later, Grim stood in his place. He frowned, snatching the card from the witch and turning it over in his hands. "What's it for?"

Shamir rolled his eyes. "I can't give you all the answers, what fun would that be?" His head tilted, eyeing Grim's nude form. "Pity you don't have pockets. I suspect we'll have to do something about that because you're going to want to keep it on you… Ooop." He waggled a finger at Grim. "No spoilers."

Grim glanced at the corpse, then moved to stand with Kit, tucking her under his arm. The shrill of sirens sounded in the distance. She put her arms around his waist, hiding her face against his gore-stippled chest. That last explosion had to have been seen for miles… How were they going to get out of here, never mind back to Flatts?

"What do you want, Shamir?"

Kit's eyebrow rose. Grim said it like they'd met before and he wasn't a fan.

Shamir tapped his lip, thinking. "At the moment a burger, with fries—No. Onion strings. Do you like those?" he asked Kit.

"Sorry, I'm a fry girl," she sighed, cuddling closer to Grim and too tired to do anything but go with it. "He's mad Sama locked Chanté up in the Spire and is here to piss in his wife's cornflakes."

"Sama prefers Muesli, but yes, that's the general idea, and," he patted the wad of cash he'd lifted from the corpse and waggled his eyebrows. "You fly, I'll buy…"

"Fuck, I'm game, but transportation's gonna be a problem," Brick said, coming up behind them. Kit's cheeks burned red and she looked away. If that was him cold, good Lord…

"Psh, details, but yes, I suppose I'll have to do both. Extra pickles?" Shamir asked brightly.

Brick looked at Grim. "We're keeping him."

"No, we're not."

"Whatever we do, we gotta do it soon," Deuce said, cupping his junk as he jogged over. "Looks like they got choppers coming up the Hudson." He jerked his head over his shoulder at two rapidly approaching lights from the south.

"Goddamn it…" Grim's arm tightened around Kit, and he glared at Shamir. "Fine. You sort out that little fucking transportation detail, and we're game, but being buck-ass naked, covered in gore ain't exactly gonna go over well at an Arby's. And no fucking pickles."

"Ah, Mr. James," Shamir laughed. "Pickles are non-negotiable, and you've no idea how refreshing your lack of faith in me is. Let's see if I can make you a believer, shall I?"

He raised a long-fingered hand, pressed his thumb and middle finger together.

And snapped.

CHAPTER SEVEN

GRIM BLINKED, and they were in a 1970s town car, parked at the Tupper Lake rest stop, engine running. A grease-stained takeout bag was between him and Kit.

"Fuuuuck…" Brick breathed out, running a hand over his cut and pressing back into the driver's seat. "Did I drop a tab or seventeen and forget about it? I coulda sworn we were buck naked on top of a mountain about five hundred miles south two seconds ago."

"Talking to a head case in fancy pajamas?" Deuce asked.

"Yeah."

"Unless we had the exact same fucking trip, I'm pretty sure that happened." Deuce scrubbed at his face. "But I ain't complaining. Dude did us a solid."

Kit ran her hands over her spotless tracksuit, and pulled Asorav's limp dog out of her shirt with trembling hands. "Did you know he was gonna do that?" she asked Grim, eyes wide as they slid over his clean cut and jacket.

"Nope," he said, popping the 'P.'

"Remind me how you got in good with that guy?" Deuce asked, rummaging through another takeout bag. He pulled out a burger and passed it to Brick. "Extra pickles."

Kit looked at them like they'd sprouted second heads. "You seriously gonna eat that?"

"You better believe it, babydoll. Mmm. Nice." Brick picked

off a pickle and dangled it between the seats. "Want one, Grimmers?"

—*!!*—

[DISGUST]

"Fuck off," Grim growled, batting it away. Shit freaked his cat out, and the asshole knew it. "You know that arms deal Clay made with the witches after shit hit the fan with Cantone?"

"The one you passed the fuck out in the middle of?" Brick quipped around a mouthful.

"He did what?" Deuce looked between them. "Why the hell didn't I hear about that?"

"I didn't fucking pass out. Shamir showed up, spewed a bunch of fucked-up shit, then the next thing I remember, I was riding back with Stitch."

Brick nodded. "Yeah, 'cause you passed out."

"Listen, asshole, I didn't—"

"So what did he say?" Kit asked.

"Damn, that's good," Brick mumbled around his bite. "There fries in there?"

"Onion strings."

"Pass 'em over…"

Grim fished out one for himself and frowned, flicking the pickles off before his cat had a coronary. He shrugged. "Shamir said that she was coming."

Deuce cocked an eyebrow. "Who, Kit?"

"Yeah, I guess." Grim bit into his burger. Damn. It was fucking good, even with the ghosts of pickles past.

[GAGGING]

Get over it.

"Okay, so we're back. What the fuck's the game plan?" Deuce asked, wiping off his hands.

"Call Triss," Grim said around his mouthful.

Deuce blanched. "Why the fuck would we do that?"

"Because she's got more loyalty to the crew than MK,

hates Nikki, and would do pretty much anything you asked her to."

"Including bend over," Brick added, popping onion strings into his mouth. Deuce growled at him, and he held up his hands. "And nobody takes her seriously. If they're up to shit, they're still gonna let her go on her merry thinking she's fucking oblivious."

"You call her then."

"She don't like me, and Grim's supposed to be down for the count."

Deuce glanced over his shoulder at Kit. She rolled her eyes. "I've met her *once*. Man the fuck up."

Brick laughed, choking on his burger.

"Fine." Deuce snagged Brick's cell from the dash and dialed.

Damn. It was like the past hour had never happened. Grim's stomach churned around his burger. How much power did that asshole Shamir have?

Remind me not to piss him off.

—snorting—

Whatever. Grim snagged some of Kit's fries. "Put it on speaker."

Deuce glared daggers at him, but pressed the button. Triss picked up on the second ring.

"Hello?"

"Uh, hey—"

"Deuce! Oh my God, are you all right?"

"Um…"

"Everybody's seen the news, New York is fucking shut down, and they're saying Grim is some kind of a terrorist? I mean, duh, it's bullshit, but the Feds have been at the clubhouse all night taking stuff out, and they had a frickin' triad of Blēda with them! Are my mom and dad with you? Is everyone else all right? Where even are you?"

"Uh… where are you?"

"Me?" Her voice dropped and got husky. "I'm in bed, thinking of you and touching—"

"Triss!" Deuce hissed, going scarlet. Brick bit his knuckle, just about pissing himself.

"Oh my God, am I on speaker? Shit. I'm on speaker. Hi, Mom and Dad! And I was gonna say, I was touching the Bible. Hellooo. I pray for everyone in the club first thing in the morning. No better way to start the day than with a hallelujah."

Deuce's throat bobbed. "A hallelu—"

Grim smacked the back of Deuce's head and mouthed, "Vote!"

"Um, thanks, I guess... Uh, hey, Triss... did MK say anything about the vote?"

"Psh... yeah, and I am so frickin' mad about that! Miser was all 'you gotta postpone it' and MK was all 'no, the club won't stand for that,' " she mimicked. "and, how 'it's more important than ever we have a prez now,' and then he went off about how Miser needed to shut up 'cause he was so hot to have this vote about exiling Nikki in the first place..."

Brick scribbled something on the takeout bag and held it under Deuce's nose. He glanced at it and batted it away.

"...God, she's such a fucking—"

"Um, yeah. So, where are they havin' it if the Feds are at the clubhouse?"

Triss buzzed her lips. "Your guess is as good as mine, I mean, mine is probably better, but I don't have anything I'd put money on. All I know is after you guys left, things around here got weird, but you don't wanna know about that..."

"Why don't I wanna know about it?" Deuce snapped, a muscle in his jaw popping.

"Welll..." she drawled out all coy, "Last night I hooked up with Riff—"

"You what?!"

"Oh my God," Grim smirked at the eye roll in Triss's voice

and the vein popping out of Deuce's forehead. "Not like hooked up, hooked up, I mean, not that it's any of your business or anything, I totally could've if I wanted to, but— why am I even telling you this? Ugh, anyways, we went to the pool hall in Benson and there were a lot of guys from Satan's Vengeance there. Nobody big, just like prospects and stuff, but it was a super weird vibe."

Grim exchanged looks with Brick and Deuce. Benson was firmly in their territory; there shouldn't have been anyone from SV there, prospects or no, and if there were, they sure as hell shouldn't have left breathing.

"Weird vibe like how?" Deuce growled.

"I dunno, like everyone was just kind of eyeballing each other, and then Riff told me to hang tight and went into a back room with a bunch of them—"

"He left you by yourself?!" Deuce's fist clenched, his features blurring and beginning to shift. Grim and Brick edged back in their seats, exchanging looks. Fuuuck... Man was losing his shit...

"Um, yeah," Triss said, oblivious. "But only for like a half hour, and then we left."

"A half—You stay the fuck away from that asshole," Deuce growled, tearing at his hair. "You hear me, Triss?"

"You gonna come make me, Daddy?"

Deuce let out something between a growl and a roar and slammed his fist into the console. "Yeah. Where the fuck are you?"

"I-I'm at the vet's, but—"

"Rockwell still there? You're not alone, are you?"

"No, he's got another hour before he's released, and Mouse set up shop in the galley right before the Feds came, but, Deuce—"

"Tell Rockwell I said he's on duty. He stays with you, and Mouse stays put, too. Lock the fucking door and don't let anyone in or out until I get there, you understand me?"

"I—"

"Do. You. Understand. Me?" he gritted out.

Triss sighed. "Yeah, but shut up a minute. Feds have got unmarkeds rolling through town, and Mouse says there's eyes outside."

Deuce's gaze flicked to Grim's, and he nodded. "On it. I'll be there, Triss, just hang tight."

"Okay," she said, suddenly sounding very small.

Deuce cut the call, knuckles white around the phone. "We gotta get her out of there. If any of our guys are in bed with SV, between the arms stockpiled and other shit Doc usually sits on, the vet's one of the first places they're gonna hit when shit goes south."

Brick scrubbed a hand over his face. "Agreed, but the question is, where the fuck do we put her and Kit while we blow shit up? If the vet's compromised, so's the warehouse and any other business we got a toe dipped in."

"Mama Roe would watch 'em," Deuce said after a long pause.

Grim groaned, pointedly not making eye contact with the guys. Yeah, she would, but no way they could ask her… especially not him.

"Who's Mama Roe?" Kit asked.

"Doc's sister. She runs the battered women's shelter in Fulton," he said, scratching his stubble. Damn. Wasn't his first choice, but then again, none of this shit was. Woman would definitely protect Kit and Triss, and the Sanctum was a goddamned fortress.

"Hates men," Brick added, finishing off the onion strings.

"She's got just cause after what after what SV did to her daughter," Deuce shot back.

"I ain't stating otherwise, just presenting the facts…" Brick looked at Grim in the rearview, his eyes hard. "You there for that?"

"Yeah," he muttered. "S'what got me put on probation with the club."

Kit pulled back from him. "Why, what did you—"

"Not a fucking thing," he growled, raking a hand through his hair. "Shiv and Grapple... assholes cornered Mama Roe's daughter in an alley. By the time I came out... It wasn't fucking good. I called it in, but it was too late. When Reaper found out I narc'd, he lost his shit."

And when Grim had refused to do a job to get back into SV's good graces, he'd ended up locked in the clubhouse's fucking basement for two plus years, feral as fuck and servicing mollys.

[SHAME]

Grim's knuckles popped. *Not on you, buddy.*

"Not the way the media played it," Brick muttered.

"Yeah, no shit. Grapple and Shiv made sure of that." Clay had almost bankrupted the club sinking the charges against Grim for aggravated rape and murder one they'd pinned on him.

Doc had never believed their shit, but Mama Roe hadn't been convinced and made it her personal mission to fuck over both MCs whenever possible. Woman was loud and had enough pull with both the human and shifter communities to make shutting her up problematic. The entire town of Fulton was a no-fly zone for anyone in a cut.

"Not the way the media's playing this shit show, either," Deuce said, grimacing. "Look, we don't gotta escort them to the door. They just gotta show up and say they're on Reaper's radar. Mama Roe'll be all in." His stomach gurgled. "Shit... I shouldn't have eaten that..."

"Um, what if I'm not all in?" Kit said, crossing her arms under her tits and plumping them up.

—want—

Yeah... "Look, we can figure it out after we snag Triss..."

Grim deflected, not even trying not to stare. Damn, she had a gorgeous rack. He wet his lips—

"A frontal assault ain't gonna work, which leaves the hatch," Brick said, putting the cage in gear and backing up. "Should throw off the Feds, but MK knows about that shit, and he's probably not keen on us making off with anything."

Grim grunted his agreement, still eye-fucking Kit. She'd lifted his ring from between her tits and put it to her lips, looking out the window. Goddamn, she was beautiful... He ran a hand down his jaw, trying to focus on what the guys were saying.

"You really think he's got someone watching the hatch?" Deuce asked. "They think we're still in the city."

"Dunno, but I feel bad for the poor fuckers if he does," Brick laughed.

Kit scowled at them. "You guys gonna clue me in, or keep talking like I'm not here?"

Grim put his arm around her. She'd only eaten half her burger and a couple of fries. "You should finish that."

"Not hungry."

"Maybe not now, but no telling when you'll see anything else."

She shot him a look and jammed a fry in her mouth. "Happy? Now spill."

No, but... "The hatch is the emergency exit to the vet's. Only Doc and whoever's got a seat at the table know about it. Comes out in a fucking swamp."

"It's about two and a half klicks southeast of where that piece of shit house was," Brick said, turning onto a backroad.

"Not quite two miles," Deuce translated, giving Brick some serious side-eye. He winced as his stomach gurgled again. "Tell me you're not gonna be a fucking problem."

"I'm not gonna be a fucking problem," he parroted back.

Grim and Deuce both snorted. Without a doubt, Brick was gonna be a fucking problem.

KIT PLAYED WITH ANOTHER FRY, absently teasing it under Cecelia's nose. The little dog didn't so much as twitch. "Great," she muttered. Burned down or not, she didn't want to be within a hundred miles of that house, never mind two.

Grim tightened his arm around her, staring down her shirt again. She rolled her eyes, biting back a smile.

—Girl, stop it. You want him to eat you as bad as he wants to snap you up.—

With Deuce and Brick in the car? No frickin'—

He planted a kiss on her forehead and started stripping.

Kit's breath caught. Sweet baby Jesus.

—Mmm. You sure about that? Why not give them a show? Making those two toms drool over what they can't have would be hot as fuck. And that big one needs to learn his damned place.—

Her breath caught, nipples tightening into points. *I—*

—Do not even try to lie to me right now, Katherine.— Kat growled.

Grim's Henley came up over his head, tatted abs rippling in the moonlight. Kit ran a hand over them, teeth pinning her lip. "Any particular reason you're getting naked?"

—Yeah, cause you about to get busy.—

"Shifting in clothes sucks… and the way your tits look in that fucking shirt's killing me." Grim's fingers tipped up her chin and his mouth was on hers. Soft, then seeking. "Let me in, baby…" he murmured, cupping her nape.

—That's my girl… go get you some…— Kat purred.

Kit opened for his tongue, and he swallowed her moan. She pressed her thighs together, so Goddamned turned on, palm sliding up over his pecs. Damn, what this man did to her…

She glanced at the front seat, flushing with heat. Okay, maybe Kat was right and a little bit of that was because the guys were in the car.

—Try that again.—

Okay, fine, a lot of it's because they're in the car.

[SATISFACTION]

Grim took her hand and put it on the hard length straining against his jeans. Guess he liked having an audience, too. Kit drew in a sharp breath, her panties soaking clean through. He growled low in his throat, and scooped Cecelia from her lap. "Hold this," he said, dropping the dog into Deuce's.

"Are you fucking kidding me?"

"I hope not," Brick said under his breath, adjusting the rearview.

"Grim—" His lips claimed hers again, cutting off her half-hearted protest as he pushed her down onto the wide bench seat. Kit's fingers curved around his shoulders, lost in the feel of his mouth on hers. Goddamn, the man could kiss...

"You gonna listen to Kat and let me fuck you, baby? 'Cause I really wanna fuck you, and she's right, that son of a bitch needs to see you're mine."

YOU TOLD HIM!?

—Psh. No. But I might have said something to Darke...—

I can not with you right now.

—Then do something with your boy. He's waiting for the green light.—

"If it gets weird, we can stop..." Grim's hand skated along the bare strip of skin at her waistline, working the tight shirt up to just under her breasts. He raised an eyebrow, and she glanced at the front seat again before giving a little nod.

"That's my dirty girl," he murmured, pulling her shirt the rest of the way up. Her nipples hardened, peaking until they ached for his touch. Grim tweaked one, rolling it between his fingers with an approving growl before replacing them with his mouth. Kit fisted his hair, arching against him, feeling Brick's eyes on them in the rearview, her panties totally ruined.

"Goddamn, she's got nice tits. Deucey, you see those?"

He grunted, and Kit's cheeks heated. Oh God, was she really doing this?

—You seriously askin' that question?—

"I can smell how wet you are, Kitten," Grim murmured, nuzzling up under her jaw, his breath hot on her throat. "Such a dirty, dirty girl getting off on them watching." He tugged on her nipple, and she whimpered, the sensation shooting heat through her core. His scruff rasped across her skin with his smile, and he pushed up, hands at his belt. "Take off your clothes and bend over."

Kit glanced at the front seat. Brick was still driving, albeit a hell of a lot slower than before. Deuce had turned in his seat to watch. She blushed, taking off her shirt and wriggling out of the pants.

"That's it, baby…" Grim's nostrils flared as she got on all fours on the back seat, running a hand over her ass and between her sticky thighs. "Goddamn, you're fucking beautiful… spread those legs for me…" His hands cupped beneath her ass, thumbs opening her wide.

"Jesus Christ, she smells like fucking candy," Brick muttered, adjusting himself in his seat.

"Mmm," Grim murmured, ignoring him, "now play with that pussy before I taste it."

Kit buried her face in the seat, breath hitching as her fingers swirled around her clit, then found her moist center, sinking in.

"Fuck, that's sexy," Brick murmured, licking his lips. "Go deeper, babydoll."

She moved her fingers to comply, and Grim's belt buckle clinked. The hiss of leather against denim filled the air, then cracked down against her ass.

Kit yelped, and before she could draw another breath, the belt landed across her other cheek. She raised up onto her knees with a cry, and Grim pulled her back against his chest, cruelly squeezing her breast.

"You're *mine*," he snarled into her ear. "Your pleasure, your punishment, and this pussy all belong to *me*."

The belt flicked against her clit, and she yelped again, breathing hard. *Oh God, that shouldn't be so hot… Why is that so fucking hot?* Her cunt throbbed, dripping for him.

—*Because they're goin' full alpha on us, girlfriend.*— Kat said, all breathy.

What do you mean, they're—

"You don't listen to him, you listen to me, understand? He can look all he wants, but I won't fucking share you. *You. Are. Mine.*"

His cock thrust between her legs, spearing into her, and Kit cried out, reaching back. Her fingers tangled in his hair, pulling him close.

"Say it," he panted against her throat, the sharp tips of his teeth scoring her skin as he nipped at her.

"I'm yours…"

"Again."

"I'm yours!"

He pushed her back down, gripping her hips and bucking into her, punishing her with his dick. Kit braced against the car door, tits slapping together with the onslaught, her head going light—

Grim pulled out, flipping her onto her back, legs over his shoulders and his face buried in her pussy. Her eyes rolled up into her head as he lapped and sucked. Her walls tightened around his thrusting fingers…

He slapped her clit, and she moaned. "Did I say you could come?"

"Please, Grim…"

He slapped it again. "Did I say you could come?"

"No, but…"

"Get on your knees and suck my cock."

Kit bent forward and lapped around his weeping crown before taking him in her mouth, pre-cum coating her tongue. He fisted her hair, hips pumping up. She gagged at the invasion, throat burning.

"Fucking take it. That's right. You like the way you taste on my dick, don't you?"

She hummed her assent, tearing up, her cunt throbbing and so damned empty…

"Deeper, Kitten, open that throat for me… Yeah. Fuck, that's good…" His head fell back, and he groaned, pumping into her. "Jesus fuck… come here…"

He pulled her off his cock to straddle him and wiped away her tears. "Does it hurt?" He asked, kissing her softly. His thumb dropped to strum her swollen clit. "You need me to fill up this pussy?" She nodded, and he kissed her again, hands caging her hips. "Take what you need, baby."

Kit notched him at her entrance, slowly slicking down his thick shaft. God, the stretch and burn of him… her head tipped heavenward and his lips captured her breast. Kit moaned, rocking and raising up. Feeling him hit so fucking deep inside… She fell forward, burying her face in the crook of his sweat-streaked neck, losing herself in the rhythm of his hips.

He shoved two fingers into her mouth. "Suck. Get 'em nice and wet."

Kit complied, moaning around his digits. Grim growled his approval, reaching around her and parting her cheeks.

"You know how bad they wanna tag team you right now?" He murmured into her hair, slick fingers skating over her pucker. "Him and Deuce are dying to pull their dicks out, watching me slide in and out of your juicy cunt, imagining it's theirs."

"Jesus fuck," Brick growled. "This is payback for being an asshole, isn't it?"

"*Watch*," Grim growled, the power of his alpha command

echoing through the car. It coasted to a stop on the side of the road. Brick turned and gave them his full attention, his expression strained.

One finger breached her backside and then another. Kit moaned, tipping back to accept them. "Mmm, that's my filthy kitten," Grim murmured. "Lean forward and show them how that pretty hole stretches around my fingers while I fuck you."

Kit's walls clenched, a wave of slickness dripping past him, down her thighs. "Oh God, please Grim, let me come…"

"Not. Done. With. You," he grunted, punctuating each word with a thrust, battering her core.

Kit's pussy tightened, squeezing his rigid length. Tears pricked at her eyes. "I can't—"

"Fuck, you can. Fucking take it."

"Grim—" she whimpered, her nails digging into his shoulders. Her teeth found the crook of his neck and she bit down, his sweat tinging her tongue. The urge to bite him flared through her, and she went to pull back—

His hand cupped the back of her neck, pressing her to him. "No. Don't stop—"

—BITE HIM—

Her cat's insistence shocked her, and she paused. *I—*

—DO IT—

Sweet Jesus… Kit's teeth sank into him, elongating, the motion no longer her own, but so frickin' right… He moaned, eyes rolling back in his head, cock swelling. Salty copper stained her lips, sending her heart racing.

—Yasss… now, Boy Vengeance…—

Grim's hands dug into her flesh, the cords of his neck rigid as he threw back his head.

"Fuck Kit, you feel so fucking good… I can't…" His forehead snapped to hers, his gaze drilling into her soul. "You're *mine*." His pupils waffled, voice burled with a weird binary resonance. He licked a trickle of his blood from her chin. "Tell me you want this."

"Oh God, I want all of you," she panted, the same dual echo in her throat.

Grim let out a low growl and something stabbed into her core. She gasped, pleasure erasing the sharp pain, and a sensation like a flower opening filled her. The scent of cinnamon and citrus filled the car, and the men groaned. Grim licked his lips, a satisfied smile flitting over his face. "That's it, baby, ride it…"

"Fuckin' A," Deuce panted, his knuckles white around the headrest.

Brick's chest heaved, his eyes huge, struggling against Grim's command to watch. "Bastard. You fucking bastard…"

—Mmmm—

"MINE," Grim growled over her shoulder. The alpha command sent the two men reeling back, and Deuce whimpered.

Kit's breath stuttered. Holy fuck, that was fucking sexy… Her nipples peaked to painful points, her pussy tightening like a vise around his driving shaft…

"Goddamn… Come for me, baby, rain all over my cock—"

Kit cried out, and Grim captured her mouth with his, sucking his blood from her tongue and groaning as he devoured her. A dam burst, waves of pleasure rolling through her as hot spurts of his ejaculate seared into her womb. Her cunt clenched at him, the aftershocks of her orgasm rippling over his pulsing dick.

"Mmm. That's it baby, take all of it," he murmured, stroking her sweat-slicked back, lips feathering kisses at her temple. Kit's vision swam, and she collapsed against his heaving chest, limp.

—Dayum, girl.—

Mmm. Kat could say that again. That'd been fucking intense.

—Um, so you know he just barbed you, right?—

Kit's eyes popped open. *I thought you said no.*

—Yeah, but look, Boy Vengeance is persuasive, and after what that vamp said? If there's a way to get out from Reaper's thumb, we need to jump on that shit.—

Kit's pulse pounded in her ears. *By getting pregnant?! On what fucking planet is that a good idea? Hellooo, homeless, no job— oh, and people wanting to kill us...*

—Which is why we need to hurry up and get this first shift out of the way. Calm down. Our boys will take care of us, and technically, they just triggered us to go into heat.—

Oh well, that makes it okay then. I mean, we didn't "technically" kill Mr. Asorav's dog, either.

—Please, that thing's still breathing, and I know for a fact they sell condoms if you're that opposed.— Kat huffed. *—It's all gonna work out fine, you'll see.—*

Grim kissed Kit's temple again, her walls fluttering over him as he softened. "Love you, Kitten," he murmured with a gentle smile, the back of his hand stroking over her abdomen.

Kit's lips tipped up despite herself. Maybe Kat was right, and it would all work out. Nestled against Grim's chest, it was easy to believe it could. And dear God, she was gonna pray like hell 'till it did... and maybe get the morning-after pill at the first pharmacy they passed.

Maybe.

"Mmm. Say that again," she breathed, tracing one of his tattoos.

"Can you not?" Brick muttered, scowling. He adjusted himself with a frown. "Totally ruins the scene."

Kit reddened and grabbed her shirt. "You're such an asshole."

"No, he's an asshole for finally taking alpha like that," Brick said, glaring at Grim. "Couldn't fucking prove it during that piss poor speech you made for Clay, could ya? Nahhh, had t'wait until you find a hot as fuck chick, then barb her fine ass in front of us. That takes 'look but don't touch' to a whole 'nother fucking level, man…"

"He's not wrong," Deuce grumbled, pinching at his nose. "Shit's harsh. You know I'd follow you anywhere."

Grim scrubbed at his face. "Wasn't like I planned it. My cat—"

"Figures," Brick muttered. "You're not half the prick he is. Whatever. It's done, and aside from that last bit, damn, babydoll, you are serious spank-bank material. That little asshole?" He pursed his lips and gripped his cock. "Goddamn, I'd tear that shit up."

"Dude!" Deuce ran a hand over his face. "Remember, we talked about boundaries? That Grim's—fuck, *our*, queen."

"No shit, otherwise she'd be riding my dick right now. See? Boundary. But just because you're imagining Triss when your hand's wrapped around your cock doesn't mean I can't think about—"

"Do we really have to talk about this?" Kit asked, pulling on her pants. Grim chuckled, kicking his the rest of the way off. She turned to glare at him. "You think that's funny?"

"Deuce's denial, Brick being Brick, or how fucking adorable you are when you're flustered?

She threw up her hands. "I dunno, all of it?"

"Yes," he grabbed his shirt and ran it over his cock and thighs, grinning at her, then lounged back buck-naked with his arms over the seatback.

Kit glared, trying not to give him the satisfaction of her checking him out. He was fucking lucky she loved him, too.

CHAPTER EIGHT

GRIM STRETCHED OUT, feeling like a new man. Issuing that alpha command then asserting his dominance by barbing Kit had changed something. Claiming her had re-cast the die and altered the dynamic between him and the guys at a primal level. He could feel it in the air, the weird tension that'd been between them since Clay's death was gone.

—you are their alpha, and her mate—

Yeah. It felt better than Grim had thought it would. Right, somehow. Stepping into his father's shoes was a huge responsibility and terrifying as fuck, but with Kit at his side… he couldn't not do it. She made it all seem like a foregone conclusion. A stupid grin split his lips as she blew a strand of hair from her face, rolling her eyes at him. Her cheeks pinked, smiling back. Goddamn, he loved her.

Brick got the car back on the road and moonlight fell over Grim's shoulder. He glanced down at the wound she'd inflicted, eyes following the stippled oval her teeth had carved into his flesh. Its bruised purple halo was already fading to green, and the tiny holes scaring over a brilliant white. He rubbed at it, relishing the tingling ache and unable to stop from grinning wider.

Grim pulled her back over to straddle his lap. "You marked me, baby," he murmured, kissing her.

"That's a good thing, right?" she purred, fingers tracing her bite.

He skated his nose up her throat, his hands cupping her ass. Goddamn, she was fucking sexy. "Yeah, and I can't wait to give you mine. That checks the box for blood, just a matter of time now."

Her brow furrowed, and his followed suit.

"What is it?"

She shrugged. "I just… back at the mountain. That witch." Kit bit at her thumb, weirdly subdued. "Kat killed him, Grim. She pushed me, I don't know, down, and came out at him. My teeth, hands, they changed, but the rest of me…" She looked up at him with big eyes. "That doesn't mean I went feral, does it?"

"No," he sighed, pulling her close. "Sometimes, shit like that will bring out attributes in shifters before they go through a full change. It's a defense mechanism, Kit. Going feral…" he ran a hand over his jaw. "You can't come back from it. Not easily at least. Your beast totally takes over."

"Trust me, unless you're Grim, you don't come back at all. He's the only shifter I've ever heard of that's done it," Deuce threw over his shoulder. "S'why they get put down. Shifter goes feral, you end up with a physically enhanced wild animal with all the cunning of a human and none of their compunctions. Shit's dangerous for everyone."

"Dude, your vocab is killin' it tonight," Brick held out his fist for a bump and Deuce ignored it. "Whatever, Deucey, you know you want to… But yeah, Grimmers is a fucking unicorn. That cunt cat of his has taken his ass for a ride twice, and somehow, he's managed to claw his way back. Damned if anyone can figure out how he does it."

Fuck, it'd been more than twice, but they didn't need to know that. Grim looked out the window, not wanting to talk about it. Kit must've got the memo, because she didn't push. The car slowed, and the enforcer spun the wheel, pulling onto a poorly maintained trailhead. Backend of the fucking boat they'd been cruising around in stuck halfway out onto the road. So much for stealth.

Brick killed the engine. "What's the plan?"

"I shift, we go in there, pack up as much firepower as we can carry and snag Triss on the way out," Grim said, going for the door.

"What about Kit?"

She'd put on his jacket and had tucked the scarf-wrapped dog back into its pocket. "What about me? I'm not staying here, and I can carry stuff, too."

"Tell me you can fire a gun," Brick said, pulling out one of his pieces and slapping it down on the center console.

She looked at it like it was gonna bite her. "Um, sure… Don't know if I'll hit what I point it at, but I can try."

"And that answers that question," Brick sighed, snagging the piece and re-holstering it. "You're with me, Deuce's got point, and Darke has our six. Cool?"

Grim's brow raised at the enforcer. For once, it was an actual fucking question.

—*as it should be*—

Grim nodded, sanctioning the plan. "Yeah, cool." *You ready, buddy?*

—*ready*—

He opened the door and dropped to all fours, letting his cat take over.

DARKE   PROWLED   THROUGH   THE UNDERBRUSH, fighting the urge to flick sludgy mud from his paws. It'd snowed while they'd been in the city, leaving an inch of soggy slush over half-frozen muck. He hated the way it squished between his toes, gritty with ice and smelling of rot.

And now the temperature was rising; the stagnant air laden with a dense fog and the pattering of melt-off punctuated by hollow thuds of falling slop. Aside from that, the swamp was eerily silent. It was that weird in-between time when night begins to give way to dawn. Darke could feel it, like a rising tide lapping at his subconscious, bringing with an awful feeling of certainty.

Something was coming with it.

A clump of the nasty white shit plopped down on him from above, raising his fur. He snarled silently at a pine limb springing back up like it was happy it'd dropped a bomb on him.

Wrong place, wrong time, his man laughed.

—*fuck you*— Darke chuffed, shaking off the sludge. He missed his nest of blankets at the clubhouse, his cave in the hills… When his mate was finally free, he was going to show her all his secret places. Chase her through them…

He growled, paw sinking dewclaw-deep into the muck.

S'up with you? his man asked.

—*want Kat*— Darke muttered back, flicking his paw. The thoughts they'd shared while their skin siblings had rutted had only made him more eager to claim her himself, and Kat felt the same. She was losing patience with Kit.

Darke couldn't fault her for it. He hated having to wait. Ached.

Aww… got blue balls, buddy?

He snarled at his man's laughter. Not happy about it, or the way their mate's bite felt. It tingled, pulsing out under his skin. Shifter venom wasn't supposed to do that; at least, he didn't think so. Maybe it was because she'd bitten him as a two-legger. They had filthy mouths. He licked at it, then stopped himself, his ears going flat. If he kept messing with it, Grim would probably have Triss give him a shot.

His fur ruffled, screaming to be groomed. Nope. Not gonna do it.

In front of him, Brick splashed through an iced-over puddle, his footsteps heavier than usual. They'd hoped this would be a quick in and out, but after the first hundred feet, it was pretty obvious that wasn't going to happen.

Kit had zero clue how to move through the frozen, sucking mire, slowing them down until Brick'd convinced her to let him give her a piggyback ride to the hatch... or maybe losing her shoe had done that. Darke wasn't sure, but he did know that as much as his man appreciated the view of her splayed ass, neither one of them was thrilled that her legs were wrapped around the enforcer.

Stop sulking and catch up, Grim bitched. *Deuce is probably already there, and between him having to shit his brains out again and Triss, I don't trust him to wait for us. Asshole could be walking into something.*

Darke chuffed his agreement, bounding over a rotting log—

His nose twitched. He snuffed at the rock he'd landed on. The lichen was scuffed on one side, and farther on... there. The thread was subtle, but definitely familiar. Darke rose up on his hind legs, front feet planted on the bole of an ash, nose about the height where a two-legger would reach out to steady themselves. What was that...

Teenaged boy, Grim muttered. *Fuck, it's gotta be Mike.*

—*Mike?*—

One of the dipshits I had tail Kit to the house. We never did find his body.

Brick and Kit were just disappearing over the rise, the boy's trail leading in the opposite direction.

Darke whined and snuffed at the tree again. The scent was fresh. —*not dead*—

No... We gotta find him. Tell Kat we'll catch up. Ten minutes.

Darke waffled, not wanting to leave his mate.

You think I fucking do? There's a reason Mike didn't come back to the club after shit went down at the house. If he can tell us for certain who the rat is...

—ten minutes— Darke reluctantly agreed, sending his thoughts out to Kat. She wasn't happy, but Kit was. Stupid two-leggers.

He followed the trail deeper into the swamp, circling back twice to pick up the boy's scent again.

Kid's smarter than he looks. A lynx's nose wouldn't be able to pick him up in this shit.

Darke flicked muck from his paw. *—lucky me—*

Quit your whining and—

Wet leaves squelched.

Darke's ears perked up, his attention zeroing in on an outcropping of stone. He crouched low, belly skimming the muck as he crept forward...

A mud-caked blur shot out from behind the outcropping, and Darke took off after it, his longer gait giving him the advantage. A mangy lynx dodged around a deadfall trying to throw him off. Darke launched over it and landed on the smaller cat. It yowled and hissed, fighting to turn onto its back.

Darke slapped a meaty paw on the back of its head, shoving the lynx's snout in the mud.

—stop—

The smaller cat went still, air tinged with the stink of its fear. *—D-Darke?—*

Yeah, it's Mike. Bring him back to the guys.

—follow— Darke chuffed, pushing off him, and heading back the way he'd come once he was sure the kid wouldn't bolt.

Mud spattered down as Mike shook himself off before bounding after Darke. *—I-I thought you couldn't—*

—can. follow—

The lynx drew up short. *—Nah. I can't go back, they'll kill me!—*

Stop and ask him who, you dipshit!

Darke chuffed at his man and stopped, turning to face the smaller cat. —*who?*—

The kid backed up, glancing around like someone was going to pounce on him —*Dunno his name, but I seen him at the Cat House...*— Kid looked around again after naming the club-owned strip joint, licking his chops like he was nervous. —*Look, man, I just wanna go home...*—

Tell him we don't give a fuck! Grim shot back, agitated.

Darke growled, trying to find words, but they skittered away from him like vermin when his man got like this. Darke chuffed his frustration, done with being the go-between.

He sprang at the lynx and bit onto his scruff, shaking him until he went limp, then dragged him through the mud like prey.

His man sighed. *Not the way to win friends, buddy...*

—*don't care. works*—

Darke paused in the shadows of a tree near the crest of the rise he'd last seen Kit and Brick at, and scanning the fog-shrouded landscape. The fur on his nape prickled, and the bite's annoying tingle wasn't the cause of it.

—*watchers*— he said to his man, dropping the kid in the muck and putting a paw on his throat to keep him still.

You think it's the Blēda Triss mentioned?

Darke ignored his man, sending his thoughts out to Kat. —*safe?*—

—*Yeah, we're in another damn tunnel. Deuce couldn't wait. You find Mike?*— Her voice was fuzzy, like it was coming from a distance.

—*yes*— He frowned down at the lynx. —*alive*—

—*Good. You on your way, then?*—

Darke's eyes narrowed, that feeling of being watched standing his fur on end. He slopped a pawful of moldering leaves over the kid, his stippled coat blending him into just another shadow.

—stay— he sent to the boy. *—enemies—*

The lynx whimpered, curling into a ball. Satisfied he wasn't going anywhere, Darke inhaled, opening his mouth to draw air over his tongue, tasting the stagnant air.

Death and magic rolled over his palate.

We go in with them behind us, we're not getting out, his man said.

—Boy Vengeance? You on your way, baby?—

A growl rumbled in Darke's chest, in agreement with his man, and stalking toward the origin of the scent.

—no. hunting—

<hr>

HUNTING? What the fuck did that mean? Kit had tried to ask Kat, but she'd snapped back with one hell of an attitude that Darke wasn't answering her. The anxiety behind the bitchy reply didn't do anything to put Kit's mind at ease. She wiped her slick palms down her thighs and glanced over her shoulder. The cement tube they were in was cleaner than the sewers, but she was feelin' claustrophobic as hell. Why did secret entrances always have to be underground?

"Issue?" Brick asked.

"Darke says he's hunting."

The enforcer grunted, not sounding surprised. "Double time, Deucey," he called up the tunnel. "Sounds like we got company outside."

Deuce swore and broke into a jog. The tunnel ended abruptly, and he reached up to jab a code into a keypad set into a manhole cover in the ceiling. It flashed, and the hiss of hydraulics echoing. He hefted himself through the gap before the hatch had finished lifting.

"Clear," he called back.

Brick made a basket with his hands and hoisted Kit up. She popped up into a laundry room. Two of the big, industrial driers were spinning at one end, and deep sinks lined the other. Deuce was already at the door leading out, his piece raised. He jerked his head, and Kit joined him.

"You stay here until we tell you otherwise. Shit hits the fan, you hit the tunnel. Wait for Darke or one of us to take you through the swamp. Do not go with anyone else."

Kit licked her lips, sweating in earnest. "What if none of you come?"

"Then you call the vamps," Brick said, shoving his fara-whatever pouch at her. Kit took it with trembling hands, tucking it into her waistband at the small of her back.

Deuce met Brick's eye, and the big man—

The door slammed open and someone barreled through. They caught Brick around the waist, pile-driving him onto the concrete floor. The two of them skidded, smashing into one of the driers and beating the shit out of each other. Kit screamed, scrambling backwards.

"What the fuck?!" Deuce swore, raising his piece. "Get off him, you psychopath!"

"Rockwell!" Triss screeched, running in from the hallway and coming to a dead stop, pigtails swaying. "Oh, it's just Brick—" She drew up short, eyes going wide, and launched herself at Deuce, wrapping herself around him like an octopus. "You came!"

"Told you I would," he said gruffly, peeling her off and holstering his gun. "Get your shit. We're leaving."

"Psh." She rolled her eyes. "Like I haven't packed yet. It's all right there in the driers. Figured you want cash and ammo, too."

Deuce blinked at her. "The driers?"

"Not the ones running, silly, but I figured if a bunch of guys showed up, the last place they'd look was in the laundry. I mean, what man does?" Kit snickered, and Triss skipped over to hug her. "Oooh! I'm so glad you're okay! I've got a surprise for you, and—" She pulled back, scanning the room. "My mom and dad aren't here?"

"We'll fill you in once we get to the cage. You assholes set?" Deuce asked Brick and Rockwell, ignoring Triss's brows drawing together.

The two men were still on the floor, rubbing various hurts. Despite Brick's blue eyes and Rockwell's skin tone being a shade or two darker, it was obvious they were related. Especially considering the way the old man was eye-fucking her.

Gross.

Brick rocked his jaw, wincing. "I dunno, you good, Pops?"

"Shit's goin' down, ain't it?" The old man slapped him on the shoulder, and Brick grunted. "Then never fuckin' better… and who might you be, cupcake?" he asked Kit, adjusting his crotch with a deep inhale. "Damn, you're ripe…"

"Kit's Grim's." Brick shrugged at Rockwell's 'what the fuck' expression like he didn't get it either.

"Yeah, she's his queen, and ours," Deuce said, grimacing. "So keep your filthy paws to yourself."

"Plenty of experience doin' that," the old man grumbled with a quick glance at Triss. Deuce growled, and Rockwell let out a snort. "Calm down boy, only thing I've done is help her pack."

Triss huffed. "After he hog-tied Mouse."

Deuce's stomach gurgled, and he bent forward, bright red. "Figure it out," he snapped at Brick, heading for the door. "I'll be back."

"Doesn't he have his meds?"

"Nope," Brick popped the 'P', helping the old man up. "Where'd you leave Mouse?"

"He's in the galley… and I'm pretty sure there's some rifax in the pharmacy." Triss's face brightened. She grabbed Kit's hand, pulling her out the door with her. "We'll meet you there in five!"

Kit stumbled after her. "Is Rockwell Brick's dad? He's the one you said got extra during the full moon, right?"

"His granddad, and yeppers. He was the club's enforcer before Brick got out." Triss pulled her down the empty hall into one of the surgical rooms and another keypad-locked door. She punched in a rapid string of numbers, and it clicked open.

Kit's jaw dropped as she crossed the threshold. It was seriously a pharmacy… Well, behind the back counter of one. Triss made a beeline for a shelf and pulled down a big-ass bottle of pills.

"Third drawer behind you, hand me two of those empty orange bottles, will ya?" she asked, dumping a bunch of pills out and counting. Kit snagged one for her. "Thanks… should be some powdered loperamide over there." She jerked her head at another shelf. "Just take the whole thing."

"This?"

Triss glanced up at the metallic pouch Kit was holding, and snagged another bottle from the shelf. "Yep, and that drawstring bag over there." Her nose twitched as Kit joined her at the table. "No offense, but why do you smell like dog?"

"Oh!" Kit put the bags down and eased Cecelia out of the jacket pocket. "She belongs to Mr. Asorav."

Triss's brow quirked. "Who?"

"Um, the Darkling, I guess…"

"Wait, *the* Darkling?" She laughed at Kit's nod. "You stole his dog? That's totally badass!"

"No, I didn't steal it, he asked me to watch her, but—Look. A bunch of shit happened, and now she won't wake up."

Triss frowned, inspecting the tiny pile of scarf-wrapped fur. "No fever, good color… Doesn't seem to be anything wrong with her," she said after a moment. "I mean, she could've had a seizure, but those don't usually last long unless it was toxicity induced. Did she eat something bad for her?"

Kit's stomach lurched, thinking about what was in that pool. "Possibly?"

Triss pulled out a sharpie and doodled on the pill bottles. "Unfortunately, I don't think there's anything we can do about it other than make sure she's comfortable and keep her hydrated. But it's only been a couple of hours, right?"

"Yeah, but—"

[PANIC]

The feeling slammed into Kit and she doubled over; the breath knocked out of her.

"Oh my God, are you okay?" Triss asked, rounding the table to hold her up.

What the hell was that? she asked her cat, her heart racing, that tearing sensation coming back from when Kat took over before. Kit pushed it down. *No no no no...*

—*Something's wrong with Darke!*—

WHAT?!

[FURIOUS PACING]

—*I don't know, fucking asshole won't answer me! Imma beat his furry ass!*—

"My cat says something's wrong with Darke," Kit panted, straightening up. "Earlier, he said he was hunting..."

Triss shoved the meds into the bag, her expression hard. "If he ran into the Blēda that were at the clubhouse earlier, he's gonna need our help. Come on." She grabbed Kit's wrist and pulled her out of the room.

Shouting echoed down the hall.

"You stupid, stupid son of a bitch!" an unfamiliar man's voice yelled. "You know how hard it was to source all those fucking parts?! The hours of code—"

"It's a laptop—" Brick drawled, totally unconcerned.

"My life, my fucking *life* was on there!"

"Dude, please. You moved from your mom's basement to the club's. You don't have a—"

Furniture knocked around and there was a bunch of grunting.

Triss growled, her eyes narrowing as they pushed through a set of double doors into a large industrial kitchen. Rockwell leaned against the wall to one side of a stainless steel prep table, arms crossed with a shit-eating grin on his face. A bunch of chairs were scattered across the tiled floor, and Brick was sitting on a fuming, whip-thin man.

"Get off him, you asshole," Triss chided, grabbing a couple of bottles of water from a case and dumping a bunch of that powder from the pharmacy into them. "You're gonna break him, and we don't have time for this shit. Kit says Darke ran into trouble. We need to get out there and help him."

"Sweet, playtime," the enforcer said, mussing the other man's hair. The tech nerd glowered up at him, his thick-rimmed glasses askew. "We cool, Mousey?"

"Fuck you."

"That's what I like to hear," Brick said, pushing off him to stand.

Triss rolled her eyes. "Where's Deuce?"

The enforcer shrugged. "Still shitting his brains out."

"Mmm." She frowned, then a wicked light came to her eyes. "It's game time, boys." She took a deep breath, her legs splayed and head down, shaking the two bottles like pompoms during a cheerleading routine, the water inside turning a funny gray green. "Get down! Get hard! Get mean!"

Kit fell back a step. Holy shit, it was a cheerleading routine.

"Oh, I'm getting hard," Brick murmured.

Triss ignored him, spinning with this weird shake that traveled all the way up her body as she raised her hands up over her head. "Let's beat that other team! Woo! To the bat cave, y'all!" She kicked her feet up behind her and took off out of the kitchen.

Was she for real?

The doors thumped shut behind her.

—Girl, they are all Goddamned psychos. Every last one of them, but she's got the right idea, we need to bounce.—

"You get used to it." Rockwell shrugged after a moment, looking at Kit.

Brick snorted, holding the door open for the rest of them. "No, you don't."

"Fuck," Mouse muttered, "Lemme grab my spare rig. Laundry?"

"You know it, brutha." The enforcer pounded on a door as they went past. "Pinch it off, Deucey!"

"Just a fucking minute!"

"Ain't got one. Shit's hittin' the fan with Darke," he called back.

"Goddamn it…"

At the hatch, Triss had emptied out one drier and was fighting to get a bag out of another. Rockwell stepped up, took it from her, then tossed it to Brick. He grunted as he caught it.

"Nice," the big man grinned, unzipping it and jamming magazines into his cargo pants. He lifted out what looked like a grenade and grinned, tucking it into his cut. "Very nice… place rigged to raze?"

"You know me, sonny boy," Rockwell grinned back, pulling a black box with wires out from beneath a sink and fiddling with it.

"Wait, you're blowing the place up?" Kit grunted, breath knocked out of her by whatever Triss had just shoved into her gut. She looked down and her eyes got hot. Holy shit, it was her Doc Martins…

"Surprise!" Triss grinned, pushing one of the smaller packs down the hatch.

"Second rule of engagement: never leave an asset behind your enemy can turn against you," Rockwell said.

Kit jammed her feet into her boots. How the heck had Triss gotten the smell of Grapple's piss off them?

—*Who the fuck cares?! Girl, we gotta get gone!*—

Did he say something?

—*No, and that's how I know the asshole is in trouble.*—

Shit. *Hold it together, Kit...* she tightened her laces with trembling hands. "What's the first rule?"

"Hit the motherfuckers harder than they hit you," Brick said, jamming a piece into his waistband.

Mouse came into the room, hefting a rucksack that made him look like he was about to backpack through Europe. "You know those aren't the actual rules, right? NATO—"

"Blah, blah, blah," Brick shoved another pack down the hatch. "Nobody cares."

Rockwell slapped the box back up under the sink. "Five minutes, boys."

"DEUCE!" The enforcer barked out.

A door slammed open and boots slapped down the hall. "Yeah, here—"

" 'Bout fucking time. Hope you washed your hands." He grinned at Deuce's scowl and dropped through the hatch. "Hit me!"

"Gladly," Mouse muttered, handing down his pack. "Be careful with that!"

"Come on, we're next," Triss said, giving Kit a push.

She took a deep breath and dropped back through the hatch.

CHAPTER NINE

DARKE GHOSTED THROUGH THE FOG, favoring his right side, the morning's first glow just kissing the tree tops. A breeze ruffled his singed fur, spiraling misty tendrils between twisted boles and laying patches of the swamp bare. Soon, the sun would burn off what remained, and he would lose what little advantage he had.

It was a fact both he and the remaining Blēda were all too aware of.

He squeezed into a cavity beneath a deadfall's roots to lick his wounds before the dawn illuminated his staggering path through the mire.

We just need a couple minutes to get our shit together.

Darke huffed, watching his flesh knit around the oozing gash. Easy for his man to say.

The first of the witch's assassins had been a quick kill, her neck snapped beneath his paws as he dropped on her from above. He'd torn out her throat for good measure, then dragged her to a deep pool and left her corpse floating face down.

The other two were proving to be more of a challenge.

Darke lapped at his chest, the fur slowly growing back where a blast had seared across his ribcage, nearly taking off his head. If it hadn't been for the sensitivity they'd gained to magic from the witch's spell at the moot, they would've been dead.

That's called irony, buddy.

—*dumb luck*— Darke chuffed, fighting with a patch of fur that'd come in weird on his nape. He growled, unable to get it to lie flat. —*and Kit Kat*—

Yeah, us healing is definitely a bonus I don't think they counted on... Kit okay?

—*Kat worries*—

Not what I asked.

—*don't care*— Darke scraped his tongue over the roof of his mouth and shook his head, annoyed at his fur growing in wrong, and at that stupid itching tingle from Kit's bite. His muscles pinged and twitched with the unwanted distraction.

You ready, asshole? Shitheads find us here, we're fucked.

Darke took one last lick over the scab and chuffed, pushing forward—

His shoulders whacked the deadfall's roots, whiskers quivering. The hole was too small. His ears flicked back. How did it get too small?

Any time now...

Darke pushed forward again, the deadfall rising, then sinking back down.

—*stuck*—

The fuck do you mean we're stuck?

—*...*—

Idiot. Are you seriously gonna make me crawl out of—

A twig snapped close by and they froze.

Fuck.

<hr>

KIT JOGGED down the tunnel with Triss beside her, pack weighing her down. Goddamn, working at Skin had not prepared her for this amount of cardio...

—Suck it the fuck up and go faster!—

She put on a short-lived burst of speed at the frantic note in her cat's thoughts, but wasn't gonna kid herself, she was reaching her limit. Mouse and Deuce gone ahead, and behind her, Brick and his dad were catching up like they were taking a Sunday stroll, despite carrying their own bodyweight in gear.

"Hey, you closed the hatch, right?" Brick asked.

Rockwell's steps faltered. "Umm…"

"Jesus Fuck, Pops!"

Arms snaked around Kit's waist, and she was airborne, flung over Brick's shoulder as he raced down the tunnel. Rockwell laughed like a maniac, zipping past them with Triss hot on his heels.

"Why is that bad?" Kit yelled around a face-full of backpack.

Brick sped up, not answering, the static of cats talking battered the back of her mind. The enforcer chuckled manically. "When we hit, stay down, babydoll. A bunch of assholes've got the crew pinned at the entrance. We gotta get 'em clear before shit hits the fan."

"We—How we gonna do that?!"

He laughed again. "Shock and awe, babydoll, shock and awe…"

Oh, God. She was strapped to a suicidal juggernaut, and they were gonna die.

***

DARKE'S LIPS peeled back from his teeth at his mate's frantic pleas, his hindquarters bunching behind him, claws digging into the rocky soil.

—men at the hatch. Kit Kat needs us.—

His man's consciousness shook with rage, overlapping

with Darke's. A symmetry of purpose bloomed between them.

They're fucking dead.

Darke growled, pushing out from beneath the deadfall, Grim shifting their body to clear the entanglement of rocks and roots. Darke skidded on the slick terrain, lunging at the robed figure crouched a few feet away. The witch fell back, ass in the mud, and eyes wide beneath his hood. His hand raised, a sticky green glow gathering—

Darke lashed out, severing the limb and going in for the kill.

A blast of magic raked across his spine as the Blēda's steaming entrails spattered the terrain. White hot pain flared through Darke, and he staggered to face the new threat, letting out a mighty roar.

KIT AND BRICK shot out of the tunnel and took a hard left. Bullets tore into the muck behind them, raining muck and chips of granite from the hillside. Brick dove behind a low stone wall, returning fire. He pulled something from beneath his cut and lobbed it into the trees—

She was beneath him. A blast of heat washed over them from above and she screamed. Brick laughed, pushing off her, and was back up and firing, the rest of the crew diving behind the stone wall to join them.

Triss flopped down beside her, laughing. "That was awesome!"

Kit just blinked at her. A grenade… He did have a fucking—

A roar echoed across the swamp, and everything went still for a heartbeat.

—Oh, he's pissed now, girlfriend.—

Who? What the hell was that?

—That was Boy Vengeance with a vengeance—

Kit's brows furrowed. *But mountain lions can't—*

The alarm on Brick's watch went off, and a massive boom shook the ground a second later. Kit's hair whipped back, and she spun to face the entrance for the hatch, as a hungry rumbling sped toward them.

"Fire in the hole!" Brick tackled her again, and the world exploded.

THE GROUND SHOOK and Darke hit the ground, his hindquarters not responding properly. A geyser of flames erupted on the other side of the rise. Oily black plumes of smoke blocking out the weak light of dawn. Sirens and car alarms shrilled from town.

Then a fireball lit up the sky from the direction of the hatch.

Fuck, Kit!

—fine— Darke growled, unable to rise, his eyes not leaving the remaining Blēda's.

The witch's knuckles tightened around a wicked dagger as he picked his way over the trembling ground.

"Interesting," he murmured, stroking a hand over his ratty goatee, head cocked like Darke was a science project. The witch dropped to a crouch in front of him. "You'd think your spawn would've inherited the same ability to mutate under duress..."

Darke snarled at the mention of their offspring, one of his toes twitching as his spine knitted together, nerves and muscle joining where they'd been severed by the witch's blast. A growl rumbled in his chest...

Play dead until he gets closer, his man gritted out.

"Ah well, Sama will have plenty of time to see what

makes your corpse tick." He gave a nasty smile and changed his grip on his dagger, leaning forward—

Darke lunged, maw wide, fastening around the witch's skull. The dagger swiped across his chest, leaving a burning line of fire in its wake. He crunched down and gray matter spurted; the dagger falling to the ground. The Blēda thrashed, then went still.

Arrogant fucker.

Darke spat him out, struggling to rise. He turned to survey the damage the witch's blast had done to his back. Before his eyes, the jagged lines of oozing flesh above his hips scabbed over into a lightning spray of gnarled, pink flesh.

So fucking weird…

—more lives gone— Darke clambered to his feet, sides heaving. He staggered over to a muddy puddle, lapping at the muck. Witch brains tasted terrible.

You know that's bullshit, right?

—then you eat them—

No, asshole. I meant about the lives.

—don't want to find out— Darke licked his chops, ears twitching at the sound of a car starting close by.

Shit, that's the fucking town car, his man said. *Kit in it?*

—no— Darke chuffed his annoyance, trotting toward the trailhead.

***

KIT CRAWLED out from under Brick, her ears ringing. He groaned, rocks from the stonewall tumbling off him. Deuce was leaning against the cliffside.

"I don't get it…" Triss frowned, failing to find a wound to account for all the blood on his face. He pushed her away to join Rockwell and Mouse, looking out over a blackened, smoking crater on the other side of the wall.

The old man grunted and came over to help Brick up. He

slapped his grandson on the shoulder, sending up a cloud of grit. "And that's why I didn't close the hatch."

"Sure, Pops." Brick snorted, stumbling and fingering his ear.

"He loves it when a plan comes together," Deuce quipped.

Triss bounced, clapping her hands. "Oooh… are we playing *A-Team*? I wanna be Murdock!"

"Psh, Mouse is Murdock. You gotta be Amy," Brick drawled. "Too bad we left the van in Terrytown. Let's hope the cage is still at the trailhead."

"What?! No, Amy sucks, she didn't even make it through the second season!"

"And I'm obviously Face," Mouse sniffled like he had a cold, hefting his pack. His eyes had gotten all puffy.

Everyone but Kit laughed. "What are you guys talking about?"

Their attention snapped to her.

Triss's mouth opened and then shut before she spoke. "Haven't you ever seen 'The A-Team?' Like, not the remake— that sucked—the 1980s version."

Was she for real? "No…"

"Oh my God! Girl's night!" She fist-pumped the air and looped her arm through Kit's, steering her through the smoldering pit. The residual heat of the blast seeping up through the soles of their shoes. "You like butterballs? I make a great butterball."

"You don't make butterballs, you make liquid hangovers," Deuce muttered.

She grinned at him over her shoulder. "Is that why you won't drink with me?" she asked, batting her eyes.

"Yeah, that's why," he muttered, pushing past them to take the lead. He kicked a smoking boot from their path and a foot fell out. Kit looked away, her stomach churning. How many people had been out here, and who the heck were they?

In the distance, an engine started.

Is that Grim?

—Nope, but Boy Vengeance is on his way.—

Shit. "Um, guys?" Kit said. "That's not Grim in the car."

Brick swore, and she was airborne again, her gut bouncing over his shoulder as he tore through the swamp. They came to the trailhead just in time to see the town car pull out, and Darke, way larger than she remembered him being, land on its hood, letting out another one of those roars he shouldn't be able to make.

The crew froze in shock.

—Girl, I think my ovaries just exploded. Heyyy…—

The lion's massive head cocked toward them and chuffed at her in a total "S'up?" move before focusing back on the terrified kid behind the wheel—wait a minute…

"That's Pornstache!"

"The lion?" Brick asked.

"No, you asshole, put me down." Kit wriggled to the ground. "The lion's Darke, Pornstache is the one stealing our car." They were all looking at her like she was the crazy one. What had Grim said his name was? "Mike. The missing kid."

That got a reaction.

Brick's jaw tensed, and he stalked over to the car. Yep. Definitely clobbering time. Kit trailed after him with the others.

How the hell did Darke get so big?

—You're the one that bit him and thank you for that. Mmhmm. Me-ow.—

Kit's pack dropped to the ground. *She'd* done that? Hold up, but Kat had been the one to tell her to bite him. *Did you know that was gonna happen?*

[QUASI GUILT]

—You know how the vamp queen had ears?—

The trunk popped open and Kit handed Mouse her bag, one eye on Brick intimidating the fuck out of Pornstache. *Among other things, yes…*

—Claymore's cat said something once about the last queen being able to enhance someone's inner animal, and Aryanna was definitely a sly bitch.—

Kit chewed her lip. *You think the last shifter queen pulled that out of her? I figured it was a spell or something, but maybe that's why Aryanna had her killed…*

Kat didn't answer, the heated buzzing static of her talking with Darke filling up the back of Kit's skull. She rubbed a temple, and strong arms wrapped around her.

"Get in the cage, baby," Grim said, pressing a kiss to her forehead.

"I didn't know that would happen," she said, tears threatening.

Grim laughed, grabbing his jeans from the car and shoving his legs in. "I don't give a fuck, and you saved my ass more than once out there." He zipped his fly. "My cat's not thrilled he's got a cowlick, but he'll get over it… think he's gonna go full blown savannah-type lion?"

"I-I don't know…" *Do you?* she asked Kat.

—If he does, I ain't gonna be mad. A queen needs her king.— She preened.

Kit rubbed a temple. Sweet baby Jesus, her inner cat was out of frickin' control. She focused on Grim. "You're really not mad?"

"Why, because you accidentally made my lion even more badass?" He slid into the car and patted his lap, everyone packed in tight.

Well, when you put it that way…

Kit climbed in, and Brick started down the road, a filthy, miserable Pornstache sitting between him and Deuce. He didn't look any happier, but that probably had something to do with Triss squirming around on his lap. She handed him one of those weird bottles of gray water, and he grumbled his thanks before chugging it with a couple of pills she doled out for him.

She winked at Kit over his shoulder. Girl was straight-up trouble. "Cecelia okay?"

Shit. Kit pulled the little scarf-wrapped dog out of Grim's jacket, and Triss took her.

"I don't get it…" she murmured, looking the tiny Pomeranian over. "You'd think she would've gotten squished or something after all that…"

"You've had a dog in your pocket all this time?" Mouse said, sneezing. "Fuck, no wonder I feel like shit."

"You allergic?"

"Severely," he said, his voice going husky. "Chuck the fucking thing out the window."

Triss glared at him, handing Cecelia back to Kit, and she tucked the dog away, moving to sit against the car door, instead of having her back to Mouse. He scowled at her, eyes glassy and looking terrible.

"So, you wanna tell the class why someone wants you dead, Mikey?" Brick asked, smacking the kid in the back of the head when he didn't spill. "Wasn't a question, shithead."

"Gah! Said I dunno! Maybe 'cause I seen that dude pop off three fuckin' people?"

"Try again." The enforcer spun the wheel, turning onto a dirt road. "What was he doin' before that?"

"I done told you already, was on his cell talkin' about the vote," the kid muttered.

"What dude and what vote?" Rockwell asked, taking out a switchblade and flicking it. Kit sighed. Guess she knew where Brick had picked up that delightful habit.

"That dark-haired guy. He come around the Cat House, dunno know his name."

The old man pursed his lips. "So what'd he say?"

"Somewhat about havin' the vote for prez at the ol' courthouse, which don't make no sense. He ain't Mayhem, and vote's always at the club."

Rockwell grunted. "Vote aside, with all the construction,

that burned-out husk's not the worst place they could've picked, 'specially with the Feds up our asses."

"Yeah… This dark-haired guy—he have an ugly-ass snake tattoo around his throat?" Grim asked like he already knew the answer.

Pornstache turned around to look at him. "Yeah, you know him?"

"Yeah," Grim growled. "That was Shiv."

"Your brother?" Kit asked.

Mouse sneezed, and Grim frowned, giving a little nod. "Shit tracks if Reaper and Grapple were there. Assholes are joined at the dick."

"What don't track is why SV's VP was on our turf, talkin' about our vote," Rockwell muttered. "He say anything else?"

"Uh, nah. That's when Sarah an' Justin showed up. Made right quick work of them, then Pete… dumb fuck was sweet on her and ran out to help. Never even got a shot off." Mike licked his lips. "S'when he saw me, but I bailed into the swamp."

Grim frowned like something about that bothered him, but he stayed quiet.

"You know what time the vote is?" Deuce asked.

"Oh! I know! I know!" Triss squealed, bouncing. "9 AM. It's one of the things MK and Miser were fighting about."

Everyone stared at the dash clock, silent. It was almost six thirty.

"Plenty of time to get there, right?" Kit asked.

Grim's fingers tightened on her thigh. "Not if we're gonna drop you and Triss at Mama Roe's—"

"What?! Are you guys fucking crazy?" Triss screeched, spinning around and straddling Deuce so she could look at them all. "My aunt'll have us packed off to Canada before you can blink!"

"Not the worst idea…" Deuce muttered, pushing back so his nose wasn't in her tits.

Tris sat down hard, glaring at him. "I am not goin', and you can't make me."

Deuce's knuckles whitened into a fist. "I can't, huh?"

A wide grin split Triss's face, and she leaned forward. "You wanna try, Daddy?"

"Jesus, Fuck, having to watch Grim barb Kit was bad enough, if you two start fuckin' over there, I'm gonna lose it," Brick grumbled.

"We're not fucking." Deuce said, pushing Triss back again.

"He barbed you?!" she squealed.

Kit's cheeks blazed, and she buried her face in the crook of Grim's neck, his chuckle heating a very different part of her body.

Triss inhaled sharply. "Holy fuck, he did!" She scrambled over the seat between Mike and Deuce and squeezed into the fragment of space between Grim and Mouse, crossing her legs, hands on her knees and back very straight. "Sooo… tell me all about it…"

Kit's cheeks burned. "Um… maybe later?"

"Poo," she said deflating, then smacked Grim. "And you idiot! You can't send her into heat and then ship her off. When the waves start coming, if you aren't there—"

What? There are waves?

—Hell yeah, and we're gonna ride the fuck out of them.—

Grim pulled Kit closer. "I'll be there," he growled with that weird resonance in his voice again.

"Aye, aye, Captain." Triss flinched back, saluting. "Well. Alrighty then."

"Christ, any more shit you guys want to dump on me?" Mouse bitched, rubbing his swollen, gummy eyes. "When did Grim finally man up and claim alpha?"

"If Mama Roe's is out," Deuce said over him, "then what the fuck is the plan? Courthouse is smack dab in the center of fucking town."

"I got a feeling Feds and anything else with a badge is

gonna be pretty busy processing what's left of the vet's," Rockwell chuckled.

"Do you guys blow up stuff everywhere you go?" Kit asked, ticking off her fingers. "Club V, Mr. Asorav's apartment, that mountain…"

"In our defense, none of that was actually us," Deuce said.

Brick laughed. "Yeah, shit lacked finesse. You see that fucking pit from the fireball?! How much C4 you use, Pops?"

"All of it." Rockwell shrugged. Brick eyed him in the review and his granddad chuckled. "'Sept for maybe a brick or seven… didn't want to leave you hangin'."

"Nice…" Brick grinned, breaking into a cringe-worth rendition of "It's the Most Wonderful Time of the Year." Everyone in the car groaned.

"Wait, is that how you got your road name? From a brick of C4?" Kit asked.

Brick turned to wink at her. "More like a pallet, babydoll."

Well, that made sense. And Deuce was Deuce, because, well, because. "You're Mouse like a computer mouse?" she asked the tech nerd. He nodded, sniffling… or maybe he was delirious and about to pass out. Damn, he wasn't kidding about being allergic. Kit looked past him to Rockwell. "Do you paint?"

The crew laughed. "Fuck, no," he said. "Used to work for the company, making incendiaries before they sold out."

"He built bombs," Deuce clarified, thumbs busy on Brick's phone. "Everyone's still MIA… Whatever we're gonna do, we're on our own."

"What d'you think about holin' up at the garage?" Brick asked, pulling onto another backroad. "Gets this fucking boat off the street, it's only a couple blocks away from where the meet's goin' down, and Wrench ain't here to pitch a fit."

Everyone looked at Grim, and he ran a hand over his jaw. "Not the worst idea… They're closed Mondays, office is secure. Girls could wait shit out there… Yeah, do it… but you touch one fucking screw, and I'll put a bullet in you."

Brick snorted. "Whatev…"

Kit went to open her mouth to argue about waiting, and Triss squeezed her leg with a slight shake of her head. Kit's eyebrow quirked, but she held her tongue.

—*That one's got somethin' planned*— Kat murmured.

Kit swallowed the lump in her throat, pretty sure whatever it was, the rest of the crew wasn't gonna like it.

She wasn't so sure she would, either.

CHAPTER TEN

GRIM REACHED around Kit to snag his Henley and pulled it on, his elbow smacking Mouse upside the head. The tech nerd glowered at him, and he scowled back. Cage was packed fucking solid and claustrophobic as fuck. Goddamn, he missed his bike.

"Why don't you have a road name?" Kit asked him.

The car went silent, and his pulse ticked up. "I do. It's Grim."

Her brows knit. "I don't get it."

"Sure as fuck fit before you came along, babydoll," Brick said, saving him. "What d'ya think, Deucey? Seems like a 'Cuddles' now." The crew snickered.

"Fuck you," Grim muttered, well aware that tightening his arms around Kit was proving their fucking point. She sighed, leaning back against him. Whatever. Assholes.

Brick grinned, pulling into the garage's fenced-in lot. They'd made a wide circuit around town, edging onto its streets opposite from where the vet's had been. Rockwell had been right, there hadn't been a single soul in sight since they'd crossed the city limits. Probably had to do with all the black smoke and ash billowing through the streets. Sure as fuck could still hear the sirens, though.

Deuce got out and plugged in the code for the door. He disappeared inside, and a moment later, one of the bay doors lifted. The enforcer pulled in and killed the engine. Everyone tore out of the cage like it was a fucking clown car. Mike skittered behind a tool bench, hand over his junk. Wrench probably had something around here for the kid to wear…

The bay door thumped back down, and fluorescents flickered on, lighting up half the space. Grim glanced up at the section of sputtering fixtures. Wench was gonna have a bird when he saw that. The rest of the garage was obsessively neat; all the tools and parts meticulously cleaned, stored, and put away. A vintage, powder blue bug was up on lifts, and another bay had a sports car with one hell of a sideswipe down the front panel.

"Don't even think about mixing up his bolts again," Grim warned Brick. Wrench had lost his shit after the imperial vs. US thread fiasco. The enforcer wasn't supposed to set foot on the fucking property, never mind be inside the garage. "You're lucky I'm letting you out of the cage."

"Psh. Like I'd pull the same shit twice. That's just fucking hurtful, Grimmers. Hey, you think he's got anything else to eat in here?" Brick asked, eyeing the vending machine.

"He keeps a bunch of frozen burritos in the back," Deuce said, heading for the break room. "We got time?"

"Yeah, hook me up." Grim popped the town car's trunk. He unzipped a bag, and a bunch of burners caught his eye. Nice. "Here, catch." He tossed them to the guys and pocketed one before pulling out a piece. "Girls, Rockwell, and Mouse'll stay here. Deuce, me, and Brick'll head over… figure we'll play it like we're coming in hot about SV being in our territory."

"How the fuck is that gonna work?" Brick asked, rocking the vending machine back and forth. Inside, candy and chips pattered down.

Grim slapped in a magazine and jerked his head at Mike. "We bring bait."

"Who? Me?" The kid squeaked, backing up.

"Yeah, you. Seems we found your dumb ass on the side of the road, and you filled us in on what was goin' down. Good thing you overheard all that shit."

Rockwell nodded, his lips pursed. "S'plausible."

The kid's Adam's apple bobbed. "They're gonna kill me…"

"Nahhh," Brick paused his vending machine heist to put an arm around Mike's shoulders. "That's my job if you fuck this up."

"I thought you didn't want anyone to know you were back," Kit said.

Grim kissed the top of her head. "That was before you jacked up my cat. I dunno what the fuck would happen if Darke went in like that. Besides, if we can't stop the vote, I'm gonna have to lay out my case for prez."

"Still don't understand how the fuck that happened or what she's got to do with it," Rockwell said, looking Kit up and down. She fiddled with the jacket's zipper, not meeting anyone's eye.

Grim held her closer. "She's queen."

The old man frowned. "Since when do that—"

"Not just his queen, Pops. *The* queen. I thought it was bullshit too, but check it." Brick stopped fishing bags of ill-gotten snacks out of the vending machine, and pushed up a sleeve. He flipped open his knife and sliced down his forearm before anyone could draw a breath. "Watch."

The wound bled freely for a moment, then sealed shut, scabbing over and fading from the pink of a new scar, to white, and then disappearing. Mouse's jaw dropped and Triss looked like she was going to explode, her whole body vibrating.

"Jesus H. Christ," Rockwell murmured. "Never thought I'd see the day—"

"I *told* you, Grim!" Triss squealed, bouncing on the balls of her feet. "We *did* have a queen out there, and you *did* find your true mate! I can't believe it's the same person! Oh, my Gawd, you're gonna have such cute babies!" She put a hand to her chest, her eyes fluttering back, then sprang forward, fisting his shirt. "Tell me I get to be an aunt! I *need* to be an aunt!"

Grim ran a hand up the back of his neck, looking at Kit. She raised her hands, backing away. No fucking help there. "Uh… you get to be an aunt?"

"Yesss…" Triss fist pumped, spinning at Kit. "Hey, what do you think would happen if you bit me?" Kit's eyes went wide, and Triss clasped her hand together. "What if I went all *Thundercats?* I always wanted to be Cheetara…"

"I get dibs on Panthro," Brick called over his shoulder, back to rummaging for snacks.

"Idiots," Rockwell muttered, ambling off. "I'm checking the perimeter. Mouse, you setting up in the break room?"

"Yeah…" He grabbed his rucksack and sneezed, wiping a finger under his nose. "Unlock it for me, Deuce?"

Triss skipped after them. "Ooh! I'll man the microwave!"

Kit sidled next to Grim. "What is with their obsession with 80s TV?"

"We didn't get internet up here until like five, ten years ago. Local channel didn't have much in the way of a budget… or selection." He shrugged, running his hands over her arms. "I'm gonna need my cut back for this."

"Oh! Yeah, sorry." She shrugged out of it and handed it to him.

Goddamn, she was beautiful. Grim's eyes dropped to her tits straining her shirt. "I really like you in this," he said, letting the jacket fall.

Kit snorted, picking a twig out of her hair. "I'm filthy and it's a velour tracksuit."

"Filthy looks good on you…" His hands skated around her hips to cup her juicy ass. "And it feels fucking amazing…" He slammed the cage's trunk closed and lifted her onto it. Kit's arms laced around his neck, her thighs bracketing his. He pressed himself against her core, his nose dusting the side of hers. "You gonna give me a kiss for luck before I go and let me see how it tastes?"

"No, I'm gonna give you a kiss that'll bring your ass right back to finish the job," she murmured, fingers tangling in his hair and pulling him close. Grim's lips captured hers, sliding his hand up her spine to fist her hair, tilting her head back. She moaned as he made her open for him and accept his tongue...

"Now that's how you kiss a chick, Mikey. Take fucking notes. Way you look, you're gonna need 'em, especially packin' that," Brick said. Chip bags rustled. "Come on, let's find you some pants. Rest of this shit your virgin ass ain't ready to see."

"I ain't no virgin!"

"Psh, a two-liter bottle don't count."

"That never fucking happened!"

"Suure it didn't..." Brick said, smacking him upside the head as they left.

Kit giggled, breaking their kiss. "A two-liter bottle?"

Grim smirked. "Triss started that rumor after she caught him peeping on her."

"Oh, ew," she laughed. "But that's harsh! Poor kid's gonna have a complex."

"Girl gives zero fucks," he said, kissing her again.

"Mmm, I like that about her." Kit's fingers were at his zipper, then slipped into his jeans. Her fingers brushed down his shaft to free his hard length. It kicked against her palm, and she tightened her grip, stroking. "And I like this about you..."

Fuck, that felt good. "Yeah? What are you planning on doing with it?" He nipped at her lip, thumb dropping to circle her clit.

"I'm gonna put it in my mouth," she whispered in his ear,

"lick all around the tip, down the shaft, then suck your cock into my throat and let you fuck my face."

Jesus, where the fuck had that come from? Had to be a wave… He groaned, not about to complain. Her hand slicked across his crown, glossing pre-cum over his dick, her lips teasing his lobe. Goosebumps prickled up his nape. Goddamn, this fucking woman…

"I want you to use me, Pussycat," she purred, her mouth brushing against his. "Make me cry before I swallow your cum. Leave me aching for you while you're gone, then take me hard when you come back… no mercy…"

Yeah, it was definitely a wave. Game fucking on.

"No mercy…" he murmured, the citrus and cinnamon of her heat rising up to envelop them. He fisted her hair, the alpha in him relishing her wanton cry of pain. "Get on your knees."

She slid off the car and dropped to the oil-stained concrete.

"Hands behind your back, and open." She complied, eyes locked on his. "Stick out your tongue… Mmm… good girl." He swept his crown over its moist pinkness, pre-cum oozing from his tip. "Lap it up, Kitten. Show me how bad you want my cock."

The corners of Kit's eyes crinkled, and she swept a long, wet line from his base to his tip, laving every inch of his rigid flesh before hollowing her cheeks and sucking him into her hot little mouth.

Grim groaned, watching his thick length disappear and reemerge, glistening with saliva. His fingers buried in her hair. "Deeper, baby. I want your nose against my abs." He thrust into her, and she gagged, the tip of his cock hitting the back of her throat. Grim put a hand on the trunk and forced her head back, changing the angle. He thrust again, and she mewled as he breached her pharynx, the vibration drawing his balls up.

"That's my filthy girl, breathe through your nose, eyes on mine. Good girl. Now open that pretty throat and take me." He pumped steadily into her, ravaging her mouth. Her cheeks hollowed, tongue flat against his dick, his piercing clacking against her teeth. Tears ran from the corners of her eyes, the scent of her arousal making his cat insane.

"Fuck, you like being my little slut, don't you?" he growled. Kit whimpered, her lips tightening around him as his pace sped, saliva dripping down her chin. "I can smell how fucking wet that needy pussy is…" He pulled her off his cock and pushed her down, flipping her over and ripping her pants from her hips. "And I don't give a fuck what you said you want, I can smell the lie."

GRIM'S cock speared into her, and a yowl tore from her lips. Oh, God… He was right, she wanted this so fucking bad, needed it… He pulled her hips up, taking her hard from behind. Her core quivered around him, and he slapped her clit. Kit cried out, so fucking close…

"Did I say you could come?" he snarled in her ear, his teeth sharper than they should be. "You wanna be treated like a slut, you wait until I'm done with you, and I'm not fucking finished." He licked over the crook of her neck, growling. Kit moaned, her cunt weeping at the thought of him biting her…

—LET HIM.—

"Oh God, do it, Grim…" she panted. "Bite me, baby, please…"

His growl grew louder, and his hand slapped down on the concrete as he covered her, pinning her against him, her shoulder battering against his biceps as he railed her from behind. "So goddamn wet… I'm gonna come so deep in your tight little pussy. Gonna fill you up, make you all fucking dirty…"

His fingers moved between her thighs, rolling her clit between them. Her hips tilted back, wanting it… needing it…

—*Ride that wave, girl!*—

"Mmm. That's it, take my cock like a filthy slut." Grim's teeth scored over her flesh, fingers strumming. She whimpered, her cunt fluttering around him. "You need it, baby? Tell me how bad it hurts."

"Oh God, so bad, please…"

"You beg so fucking pretty… tell me, you gonna rain all over my dick when I cream this needy hole and breed you?" His voice rumbled out, more resonant than usual. Her walls wept desire, inner cat yowling, heat building. Sweat slicked her skin, cunt throbbing as he punished it.

"You want my cum in this greedy pussy, you ask for it…"

"Please, Grim, please give me your cum, please…"

"Good girl," He flicked her clit and stars exploded across Kit's vision, the sharp pain at her throat lost within wave after wave of pleasure coursing through her.

"Jesus fuck… that's it, baby… suck it out of my dick…" Grim groaned against her skin, his cock swelling and thrusting deep. Hot ropes of his release lashed against her womb, her cunt rippling around him, thighs dripping with the manifestation of their passion.

He slowed, rocking against her, licking at her nape as his cock softened, her pussy fluttering around him with aftershocks.

"God fucking damn," he murmured. "I didn't know you got off on that shit."

Kit laughed. "I didn't either."

"Mmm. I like it. Think I might keep you in heat." He kissed the base of her shoulder where he'd bitten her, and Kit's inner cat purred. "And I like this. You're mine, baby. By saliva, semen, and blood. My queen, my mate, and soon to be my baby-mama."

She smacked him, still not sure how she felt about that last bit. He laughed, sitting up, and riffling his—

"The fuck is that?"

Kit knelt, tugging up her pants. Clumps of silky white fur trailed from Grim's jacket into the shadows behind one of the supply racks. "Cecelia?"

Silence.

Kit bit her lip. The little dog always came when she was called and all that fur... shit, was that blood? She moved closer to Grim. "Do you think something got her?"

"In here? No. Wrench has got maximum throttle OCD. Place is stupid clean. She must've crawled out while we were busy." He stood, fastening his jeans and grabbed a shop-light from one of the benches, clicking it on.

Bright LEDs flooded the shadowed corner of the garage with light, throwing everything in stark relief—

A very naked, absolutely livid Mr. Asorav hissed, throwing a mutilated arm over his ruined face. His torso was shredded, flesh dangling in ribbons of gore. Sinewy muscle dripped from his limbs and a black hole gaped from behind his shattered ribs.

OHGODOHGODOHGOD...

—Run, girl! That ain't Mr. Asorav anymore!—

Grim dropped the shop light, grabbed Kit, and ran for the office. He slammed the door behind them. The rest of the crew looked up from their burritos.

"Issue?" Brick asked, rising with his hand on his gun.

"Yes!" Grim growled, pushing a file cabinet in front of the door.

"C-Cecelia..." Kit shook, thoughts rattling around in her skull. *That poor little dog, Mr. Asorav... What the fuck just happened?*

Mouse frowned at her, reaching for a bottle of Benadryl. "The dog? Tell me it's dead."

Kit burst into tears, and Triss smacked him. "What? Aww, Kit. I'm so, so sorry…"

She shook her head, gulping for air. "N-no… M-Mr. Asorav—"

A scrabbling thump crashed into the door, and everyone jumped up from the table.

"His heart… she really was his heart!" A manic laugh burbled from her lips on the tail-end of her outburst. *Oh my God, you were right…*

—Of course I was, now keep your shit together, Kathrine. Now is not the damned time to lose it!—

Nope. Definitely not the time. Kit let out another manic burble, everyone looking between her and the door.

"The fuck is going on?!" Brick yelled over her cackling.

Grim growled, pulling his gun and pushing her behind him, backing them into the far corner of the break room. "The fucking vamp's out there! Asorav."

"Wait, he's here? How the fuck did he get out of the Spire?" Brick's chair fell back and he racked his piece, throwing the table on its side and positioning himself behind it with Deuce and Mouse. Rockwell ran to the opposite corner, training his piece on the door.

The scrabbling grew louder, and metal squealed. Triss slapped her hands over her ears, running over to huddle in the corner with Kit. They peeked around Grim's legs, trembling. The guys trained their guns on the door, the steel slab buckling inward.

Pornstache stood in the center of the room, frozen, and Brick snarled.

"Take cover, you stupid—"

Hinges popped, and Kit screamed, covering her head as the door flew across the room, barreling into the table. It careened backward into the guys, slamming them into the cabinets. The vamp streaked through, grabbed Pornstache and ripped into his throat—

Oh my God, you're right, that is not Mr. Asorav…

—*Nope. That's pure fucking bloodlust. I'd suggest you pray that boy's got enough cc's to sate it.*—

It was horrible, but sweet baby Jesus, she hoped he did.

Grim and Rockwell fired, emptying their magazines into the Darkling.

He hissed, black mist dripping from his body to pool at his feet and spread upward. It blocked all the light from the room like a cloak. Kit coughed… her heart racing as her extremities went numb. She couldn't move… *Oh my God, we're gonna die…*

"Calm yourself, Katherine," the Darkling crooned. "I've not come all this way to make an end of you. Allow me a moment to indulge myself, and we'll chat, shall we?"

After this? He wanted to fucking *chat*?

—*Girl, get a clue. That vamp's gonna do whatever the fuck that vamp's gonna do, and you're gonna nod your damned head and look pretty.*—

A lurid, wet sucking filled the room, and Kit whimpered. Beside her, Triss was just shy of full-on hyperventilation.

"Jesus Christ, it's like a soundtrack to a fucking porno in here," Brick muttered.

The Darkling chuckled and continued to feed.

Then, the distinct sound of a body being dragged across the floor. "I won't be but a moment. Do collect yourselves whilst I freshen up. We've much to discuss."

The darkness receded, and with it, that weird paralysis. Both Mr. Asorav and whatever was left of Mike was gone.

"Are we seriously gonna wait for him to come back?" Triss whispered, breaking the silence. She made a beeline for Deuce, and for once, he didn't seem to mind her being close.

Kit's arms wrapped around Grim's waist, a sob catching in her throat. What if Mr. Asorav had gone after him?

[VENGEANCE]

That tearing sensation from before rolled over Kit, and she pushed it back down.

—We'd make him fucking sorry if Darke didn't do it first— Kat grumbled.

You honestly think either one of us could do a damned thing against that?

—I don't think anyone knows what we're capable of yet, and our boy? Once he figures out how to get out of his own way, wooo… —

Kit's brow rose at her cat's smugness, not sure if she was delusional or if Kat was clued into something Kit had missed. The Darkling would've torn them apart… or would he have? Aside from eating Pornstache, Mr. Asorav had always seemed so kind…

Grim buried his nose in her hair, breathing her in. "You'd rather chance him hunting us down if we're not here when he gets back?"

Triss bit at her lip. "Okay, fair point…"

"I-I think we need to hear what he has to say," Kit said, stepping back to look at all of them. "At the very least, I wanna know what happened to him." And if he'd seen Chanté at the Spire. Kit's brows knit. If he'd come out of there looking like that, what were they doing to her bestie?

Grim grunted and finished reloading his piece. A hard click came from the other side of the room as Rockwell did the same. Between them, all that was left of Pornstache was a small slick of blood swiped across the faded linoleum. Kit's stomach churned.

"Thinkin' we tell his dad he never made it out of that swamp," the old enforcer muttered, shoving his gun into his waistband. "Way that went down's just fucking embarrassing."

Deuce grunted, setting the table back onto its feet. "Far as I'm concerned, none of that shit happened."

"Dude, that was the fucking Darkling," Mouse laughed,

righting chairs, "and we lived to tell the Goddamned tale. That's mad bragging rights right there."

"True dat. Make sure you leave the in part where you pissed yourself," Brick said, eyeing the tech nerd's jeans.

"Fuck you, my water spilled when you flipped the table."

"Sure it did, Mousey."

Kit shook her head. "Are you ever not an asshole?"

A resounding "No" came from everyone in the room, followed by a sigh in the doorway.

Mr. Asorav stood there with blue shop towels looped around his narrow hips and then thrown over his shoulder like a makeshift kilt, hiding the ruin of his chest. He looked better than he had before, but that wasn't saying much.

"I apologize for startling you earlier. I was not at my best and, as one might imagine, rather fraught over losing Cecelia. I can promise you that my bloodlust has been sated and my ire reserved for those responsible. Indeed, I owe you quite a debt, Katherine."

"Oooh… now it's getting good." Triss plopped into one of the chairs and twirled a pigtail. "This is where you make him your bitch," she stage-whispered to Kit.

"I can assure you, I am no one's 'bitch,' Ms. Yewling."

"How did you know my name?" Triss gasped. "That's so fucking creepy! Do it again!"

Mr. Asorav sighed. "If I may?" When no one objected, he strolled into the break room like he was decked out in Armani instead of glorified TP. "Thank you." He pulled out a chair and sat, fingering Cecelia's rhinestone collar.

The crew stared at him, and he stared back.

"Say what you gotta say, Asorav," Grim growled, hand on his piece. "We've got someplace to be in fifteen."

Kit's pulse ticked up. He was gonna leave her? After that? She shot him a look, and he winced.

—*Darke says he's sorry*—

Tell Darke he's gonna be.

"I see you've been very busy gathering together your court," Mr. Asorav said, breaking the tension between them. "Wise of you."

Fuck her court, whatever that was. "How are you here?" Kit bit out, pissed at the entire situation.

"I shouldn't be." Mr. Asorav pursed his bloodless lips. "Though I shared a certain... affinity with Cecelia, I did so with the understanding that should I need to call upon it, the chances were slim either of us would survive. I'd hoped to avoid such happenstance, but... when it became clear Aryanna either wasn't willing, or wasn't able, to advocate on my behalf, I opted for the 'nuclear option' rather than continue to exist in Sama's lab." He sighed, running a hand over the little dog's collar. "Necessary, but most upsetting."

"Wait, you thought you were gonna die—um, de-animate with her?"

"Oh no, my dear. I don't believe she's dead, just... elsewhere. Suffice to say, I never should have allowed myself to become so attached, but the heart wants what the heart wants..." He cleared his throat, the motion doing things to his shredded chest that made Kit's stomach churn. She shuddered, hand rising to her lips and swallowing her threatening bile. The vamp didn't seem to notice.

Grim did, pulling her against him and stroking her hair. "Noted. Now what did you wanna discuss? Time's ticking."

"Hmm? Oh, indeed it is. Before my exodus, my captors spoke freely whilst pulling me apart. Incredibly foolish of them, but I suspect they'd forgotten what I'm capable of. You'd be wise to recall the same of Reaper and his protégés." The vamp's eyes drifted to the smear of blood on the floor. "That boy was not your ally."

Brick leaned forward, looming at the vamp. "How the fuck do you know that?"

"This place you have to be... is it the courthouse, by chance?" Their expressions must've told him he was right.

"This vote is naught but a sham to lure you to your death. The boy's final thoughts confirmed it."

Grim pulled out a chair and sank into it, drumming this knuckles on the table.

"Bullshit," Brick said. "You expect us to believe—"

"I do." The crew looked at Grim, startled, and he sighed. "What the kid said happened at the house never sat right. If Shiv'd seen him, it wouldn't matter how far or how fast he ran. Kid woulda been dead."

"You think Mike was stumpin' for SV?" Rockwell growled.

"Yeah, and I'm pretty sure Nikki recruited him," Grim muttered, elbows on his knees. "That night I blew shit up at the Cat House with her, I overheard a couple of the prospects talking. She'd had 'em watching out for me and wrapped up in all of Deacon's prostitution ring bullshit. Who's to say she wasn't pulling Mike's strings, too?"

Deuce grunted. "You really think she's in bed with SV?"

"Who isn't she in bed with?"

"Me for one," Grim frowned at Triss. "And I dunno, but some of the shit she said, that fucking bite I didn't give her… and if Asorav caught wind of this shit at the Spire, I'd say it's pretty fucking likely, considering what Aryanna dropped on us about Reaper and Sama being in cahoots."

"She's been fuckin' you over since long before her tantrum the other night." Rockwell crossed his arms over his chest. "Color me paranoid, but I ain't taking a vamp's word over a shifter's, even if she is a lyin' whore molly. Exactly what did you hear?"

"Several Blēda visited me during my incarceration to vent their displeasure over the fate of their brethren at my abode. Two of them were conversing about their recent assignment to Flatts. In particular, their job was to assure that in the event you turned up, you did not leave of your own volition. They were quite critical of the safeguards your rivals had put in place to that end, namely, the boy."

Rockwell wasn't convinced. "Seems a bit too pat… and I'll give you that Nikki's a dirty whore, but crawling' into bed with SV? Girl's smarter than that."

"Is she, though?" Triss asked, tapping her lip.

Grim scratched his jaw, stubble bristling. "Look, I would've thought so too, but—"

"Oh my God, just check her Insta feed," Kit said, a burst of heated rage running through her. She swiped a hand over her forehead, annoyed at the crew for looking at her like she was speaking a different language. "What? She posts shit constantly. I guarantee she'll put something up about all this. She won't be able to help herself, and then you'll know if Mr. Asorav is telling the truth."

"Stalker much?" Triss laughed, pulling out her phone and thumbing through it. "I knew we were gonna be besties…" Her eyes bugged out. "Holy crap…"

The crew crowded around her, staring at the little screen. Grim swore, his chair flying backward as he spun, putting his fist through one of the cabinets. "Those motherfucking… It was all a fucking distraction. All of it."

Kit craned her neck to see what'd upset him so much. It was a post from last night, the pic of two very different hands spreading what Kit assumed were Nikki's thighs. The caption read "Why settle for one man when you can have two? #whychoose #brothersdoitbetter #twinning #fuckgrimdarkejames #queennikkilicious4life"

"Huh. She really is that stupid. Think it's time to address your speciesism, Pops."

Rockwell glanced at Brick and then Mr. Asorav. "I stand corrected, and it might be at that."

"Fuck…" Deuce blew out his cheeks. "That's Grapple and Shiv, isn't it?"

Grim nodded, seething.

"So Nikki's fucking the two of them, but how the hell would they know to plant Mike by the hatch?" Deuce asked.

"You were the one wondering if they had someone watching it," Brick said. "Now you fucking know. All lines up. Nobody missed Mike cause he was already 'missing,' and who do you call when you got a shit job to do?"

"A prospect," Deuce muttered, running a hand through his hair. "Probably fed him the lie in case he ran into anyone loyal to Mayhem. Kid must've been shitting his pants when Darke showed up. No wonder the little fuck tried to make off with the cage."

"And who the fuck's left that fits that description?" Brick snarled. "Prospects are all suspect, MK's gotta be dirty, Christ, we start throwing in anyone who's fucked Nikki, and we don't have a club anymore!"

"Which is exactly what Reaper fucking wants," Grim shot back. "Ever since him and Clay fell out, Reaper's wanted to burn Mayhem to the ground, and save for the founders, nobody knows the fucking details of that shit show, myself included."

They all looked at Rockwell. He glanced at Kit, then pursed his lips and shook his head, not meeting anyone's eye. What the heck was that about? Her temper flared again—so fucking done with being out of the loop. That tearing sensation rolled through her again, and she pushed her cat down hard.

Stop it!

[FRUSTRATION]

Grim growled. "Which is why everyone thinks the clubs are beefing over some bullshit pissing match. Why the fuck wouldn't our guys want to re-affiliate with SV? We used to be the same club. Between Clay's death, all that at the moot, and Nikki spreading shit? Christ, she's been chipping away at my credibility for years. Most of the club thinks I'm shady as fuck, and after we lost the arms contract with Cantone, we're fucking broke. Meanwhile, SV's bringing in money hand over fucking fist dealing dope."

None of the crew met his eye, and he snorted out a laugh.

"Ex-fucking-actly. Working with the witches is a means to a fucking end for Reaper, and I dunno what him and those two assholes promised Nikki, but if it was a crown after Mayhem went belly up, bitch would jump on that shit. Christ, she tried pulling the same grift with Hellspawn down south before they got wise."

"Wait, she did what?" Brick asked, cracking his knuckles on the table.

"Yeah…" Grim paced, hands on his hips, staring at the floor. "You know what… let 'em have their fucking vote. Don't fucking matter. What we need is allies. Brick, give Asorav your phone." He looked at the vamp. "I'm assuming there's someone you can call to find out where the rest of our crew is?"

"There is."

Brick slid his phone across the table, and the vamp picked it up, dialing as he left the room.

"You're just gonna let 'em fuck us over like that?

Brick laughed. "Deucey, getting fucked is not on the agenda, man's got a plan, I can feel it." He gripped his cock through his jeans, and Kit blushed. He was definitely not soft… not that her panties weren't soaked clean through. Seeing Grim like this was fucking hot.

—Mmm, I told you, girl. Our boy's got it goin' on… now let me out so I can get a piece of that…—

Kit shoved her cat back down again, sweat beading up on her lip. *NO! Knock it off!*

Grim stopped his pacing to look at Mouse. "You ever turn anything up on who eighty-sixed Cantone's crew?"

Mouse squinted at him over his laptop's screen, his face still a puffy mess. He sniffled. "Nothing definite, but that was before we knew Reaper was out and in bed with the witches. You want me to go at it again from that angle?"

"Yeah. From what I hear, Cantone's hot to nail somebody to the fucking wall, but ain't gonna do it on my say so. I need to give him something that proves Reaper was behind it."

"Who's Cantone?" Kit asked, looking between them. Grim's expression went flat.

Hers went hard.

Triss grabbed her arm. "This is where we make ourselves scarce. Tootles." She waggled her fingers and ushered Kit through the door.

"The hell was that about?" she asked, shrugging her off.

Triss sighed. "Look. There's a bunch of MC 'stuff,' " she finger quoted, "Us ladies don't get involved in."

"Lemme guess." Kit crossed her arms over her chest, cocking a hip. "That's all the shady shit."

Triss shrugged. "Pretty much. Most of the members with ol' ladies will say some stuff behind closed doors, but he's never going to tell you everything. It just doesn't work that way." She glanced back the way they came and lowered her voice, a wicked light in her eyes. "But that doesn't mean we don't know about it."

Kit let her take her arm again. "So then who's Cantone?"

"He runs a big crime syndicate out of Ottawa. Mayhem used to have a regular thing running arms to them from the cartel down south, but maybe six months ago, our shipments started getting jacked. The last run, Cantone's entire crew was slaughtered. He killed the contract with us and put his territory on lockdown."

"And Grim thinks Reaper did that?"

Triss nodded. "Yeah, but on the books, he was in solitary at the pen. He's like some kind of an evil genius. We couldn't find any proof and no way would anyone believe Grim's brothers masterminded any of it. Grapple's a fucking idiot, and Shiv..." A shudder ran through her as they crossed the shop floor. "He's not, but from what I've heard, he gets distracted with his, um, pets. Without Reaper giving SV direction, their MC's not much of a threat, but now that he's out… He's really your dad?"

Kit frowned, trying to ignore Kat's yowling. "More like a sperm donor, but yeah."

"Sorry? You know it's weird, everyone thought you were dead."

"Seriously?"

"Yep." Triss pushed into the bathroom and pointed at the shower stall. "I've got some spare clothes that'll probably fit you. Why don't you get cleaned up while I grab them and your bag from the car? It's not like we've got anything better to do while they figure out a plan."

Kit looked down at the nasty tracksuit and grimaced. "Yeah, thanks."

Triss smiled and skipped off, door thumping behind her. Kit hit the water and started peeling off her clothes. Maybe all that shit Claymore had said about trying to keep her safe was true. Damn. If the last twenty-four hours were any indication of what he was trying to protect her from, dead or not, she owed the man an apology.

CHAPTER ELEVEN

GRIM GLANCED through the ruined break room doorway at the two women deep in conversation. Man, if Kit had a tail it'd be thrashing. Hopefully Triss was cluing her into how shit worked so Kit wouldn't rip his balls off before he could explain it himself.

—want— his cat growled.

Yeah, no shit. Grim wet his lips, thinking about that look she'd given him when he'd stonewalled her... Damn she was fine—

"My contact reports the drop was successful," Asorav said, coming into the room and sliding the phone back toward Brick. "Assume they'll be back in town any moment, if they aren't already. Their cell phones were disposed of prior to leaving as a precaution."

"Well, that'd be why they aren't answering. Sucks we can't give them a heads up, but they're gonna have to drive right by the vet's. If that don't clue 'em in something's going down, I dunno what will," Brick said, ripping open a bag of chips and putting his feet up on the table. "Doubt they'll head to the club when they see all the uniforms."

Grim nodded, agreeing. "Which'll put them either at the warehouse or the Cat House."

"Not all of 'em. Wrench'll haul ass here to make sure his sanctum hasn't been violated," Mouse snickered, still sniffling head cold style as he clacked away on his keyboard. "Man's gonna lose his shit when he sees how trashed his place is... Fifty bucks says he tries to put a bullet in Brick again."

"Better bet would be if he hits him this time," Deuce shot back.

The tech nerd laughed. "Dude, you're on."

"Psh. Whatev." Brick chomped on a chip, staring at the ceiling tiles. "You know, to get to either, they gotta go by the courthouse. They see the bikes, they're stoppin'."

"And tryin' to set the narrative straight ain't gonna go over well," Rockwell muttered, pushing off the wall. "I'll head over and keep tabs. Me turning up shouldn't raise any red flags. Far as anyone knows, I got discharged from the vet's before shit hit the fan and went on a bender. Crew shows, I'll fill 'em in and send 'em your way."

Grim snagged a bottle of rotgut from one of the cabinets and tossed it over. "Better smell like it then."

"Cheers boys." The old man tipped it back and ambled out the door. "If I ain't back in an hour, get your asses gone. Meantime, I'll bend some ears."

"Watch your back, Pops."

The old man raised a hand. "Same, sonny boy, same."

"And what's your plan?" Grim asked, turning to the vamp.

Asorav drummed his long fingers on the table. "Given Aryanna's inaction regarding my former plight, I can't say that I'm eager to return to her side. Nor would I imagine she'd be welcoming. Sama will be absolutely furious I've slipped through her fingers, which puts us in rather the same predicament, Mr. James. There's also the matter of the debt I've incurred to Katherine. If it's all the same to you, I believe I'll tag along for the nonce."

"The fuck is a nonce?"

"Deucey, Deucey, Deucey..." Brick shook his head. "Use

context, brutha. Asshole's telling us it's a temporary arrangement."

Grim ran a hand down his face, wondering exactly what that arrangement was gonna entail, but it wasn't like he was in the position to say no. Shit went sideways, the vamp would turn the tables and then some. "Brick, get your fucking feet off the table and find Asorav something to cover his ass."

The enforcer rolled his eyes but dropped his feet and led the vamp out into the garage. Grim grabbed the phone, steeling himself for what he had to do. He punched in a text, hoping like hell Cantone hadn't changed his number, waited a five count, and then dialed.

"The fuck you want, Mayhem?" the crime boss mumbled around his cigar, background noise putting him in a casino. "Your shit's too hot to touch, so I know you ain't callin' me for a deal."

"You'd be wrong. I got a proposition you're gonna want in on."

"S'it gonna be more tempting than the half-mil bounty you got on your head? If so, I'm all fucking ears."

Goddamn it, that was not what he wanted to hear. Grim shot Mouse a dirty look, trying to play it off. "Dunno. Could be. Depends on how bad you want the sacks of shit that nixed your crew last time we were supposed to hook up."

Cantone went silent, and Grim started to sweat.

A door slammed shut, the background noise cutting off. "That information would be worth a great deal more to me." The crime boss gritted out. "My sister's kid was on that run."

"Then I'll be in touch."

"You do that, and Mayhem?"

"Yeah?"

"You better have fucking proof."

The line went dead.

Grim chucked the phone onto the table and ran a hand through his hair. "We dig something solid up, Cantone's in, but if he doesn't like what he hears, he's handing my ass over to cash in on the bounty you failed to tell me about."

The tech nerd winced, rubbing at his puffy eyes. "Dude, before your ass showed up, mine was zip-tied to a chair. Shit dropped through the cracks. I just killed the post, but whoever's seen it, seen it. If it makes you feel better, it's not a snuff job. Somebody wants you delivered. Soon as I find out who, I'll let you know."

"Do that, and I need you to get me the contact info for Lars while you're at it. See if they've still got a contract out on Natalie Hale."

Mouse blinked at him. "You want the number for Hellspawn's prez?"

"Yeah. Clay might've butted heads with him, but he'll be hot to get his hands on Nikki. Bitch put his mate in the ICU," Grim muttered, knocking his knuckles against the table just as Brick and Asorav came back in. Vamp was decked out in coveralls about four inches too short at the wrists and yellow muck boots. "You good?"

Asorav raised a brow. "After being subjected to the Blēda and Reaper Ells' tender mercies, I shall attempt to persevere whilst adorned in cheap cotton twill."

"Reaper's at the Spire?" Brick ripped open a bag of white cheddar popcorn. "Oh, this I gotta hear."

"He was, and his performance was oddly disappointing." The vamp frowned, waving a hand at his chest. "Renaissance torture was ever so much more inventive. Not that the fire and brimstone sermon he subjected me to wasn't incredibly painful, but there's just something about a cage of rats and hot coals…"

Grim swore. Fucking Reaper. "What was the sermon about?"

"Hmm?" The vamp's brow cocked. "Oh… some nonsense about spies, the fruit of the land, and skunk pie… which I can assure you, was not part of the Jesuit diet."

"And we're back to spies…" Mouse murmured, eyeing Brick askance as his fingers flew over his keyboard. Grim winced. The tech nerd still sounded pissed about being interrogated over how Reaper had gotten out of the pen without him knowing. At this point, Grim was pretty sure Sama'd had more than a little to do with that.

"Nothin' personal," Brick flopped back down into a chair. "And for the record, you took that ass beating like a champ, Mousey. Most dudes cry way quicker."

The tech nerd grunted. "I'll add it to my resume… and FYI, net's got nothing on the vet's exploding or whatever went down on the mountain. Dark web's got a couple threads, but all of it's tin-foil hat shit. Looks like the Feds are working hard to keep this on the DL."

"Or Sama is…" Grim sucked on his lip. "When we were in the helicopter, didn't Aryanna say they were doing a press conference?"

"What? Asorav jumped at that bit of intel. "My queen hasn't left the confines of her lair since her unfortunate condition took hold. There's absolutely no way she would agree to meet Sama anywhere, let alone hold an in-person press conference."

"Coulda fooled me," Brick said, his feet back on the table. "Your foxy lady seemed pretty resigned to bending over for the witch queen before she dropped us off."

Asorav's brows knit. "What the devil is she playing at?" he murmured. "May I borrow your phone again, Sergeant Arroyo?"

"It's Brick," the enforcer bit out, glaring at the vamp.

Asorav didn't look impressed, but he inclined his head. "May I, Sergeant Brick?"

"Knock yourself out."

The vamp reached for the phone and the rumble of motorcycles approaching cut through the room. Grim pulled his gun, following Brick and Deuce out the door before Asorav picked it up.

"Stay here with Mouse," Grim bit out over his shoulder. Shit, where had Kit and Triss gone off to...

—shower—

Goddamn it. *Tell Kat to have Kit put on some damned clothes and stay put. Triss with them?*

—yes. both naked—

Grim stumbled, and Brick gave him a funny look.

Jesus Fuck! You can't... he wiped a hand down his face. *Together? I mean, not that I wanna see Triss like that, but...*

—Kat says she needs you—

Now's a really bad fucking time. Grim swore and shifted his cock, positioning himself behind the town car.

Brick's eyebrow rose. "Havin' issues there, Grimmers?"

"You tell me. My cat says Kit wants me, both her and Triss are naked in the shower, and we got incoming."

"What?!" Deuce yelped, his attention snapping to the bathroom door. He ran a hand over his crotch and licked his lips, crouching next to Grim. "Like, soaping each other up, girl's locker room kind of showering?"

"Dude, that shit doesn't actually happen," Brick snorted.

"Does in every porno I've ever seen."

"Got a thing for cheerleaders, huh?"

Deuce scowled at the enforcer. "Fuck off... but seriously, Grim, ask your—"

A scream echoed from the bathroom, and they all leaped to their feet. At the opposite end of the garage, the bay door groaned, slowly rolled upward.

—NEEDS YOU, NOW—

"Fuck! I got the girls, you two figure this shit out!" Grim yelled, taking off running. Halfway there, the door slammed open, and a topless, panty-clad Triss flew by him.

"Holy fuck, holy fuck, holy fuck!"

What's wrong?!

—STUCK SHIFTING—

Shit. Grim barreled through the door and skidded to a stop. He swallowed the lump in his throat, approaching slowly. The curtain hung askew, and water pattered out onto the surrounding tile.

And in the far corner, Kit was balled up, her body distended and shaped all wrong.

—LET ME OUT!—

No! Kit whimpered, pushing Kat down with everything she had, but the cagey bitch slipped away along with another piece of Kit's humanity. *I won't let you hurt anyone!*

—The fuck you talkin' about? Only one I'm gonna hurt is you if you don't let me the fuck out!—

And it did it hurt, so fucking bad. Kit's insides pressed against her bones wrong, lungs crushed on one side, her hands horrible taloned lumps of flesh… *No, no, no—*

A hand stroked over her forehead, taking too long to reach her cheek. *Oh God, Grim! He can't see me like this!* Her tongue lolled, jawbones mismatched. Unable to tell him to get away—

—LET ME OUT!— Her cat's consciousness lunged at her, overriding her senses and drowning her in primal need.

Stop it! I won't go feral! Kit fought against the encroaching blackness, thrashing. Foam roiled from her lips, spattering…

[FRUSTRATED ANGER]

—I'm about to if you don't let me the fuck out!—

Something slapped at her cheek. "Kitten? You still with me, baby? You need to let Kat come out. I know the first time's scary and it hurts, but staying like this is making it worse." He pulled her turgid form against him, his voice tight.

—Listen to him! You will kill us both if you don't let me finish the shift!—

I won't. I can't... the muscles in her throat slipped, cutting off her air supply. Her lungs fought to expand, chest spasming.

—LET ME OUT!—

"Kit!" Grim yelled, frantic. "You need to fucking shift!"

—You're killing us! You stupid, stubborn...—

Their voices grew tinny... distant. A tunnel extended before Kit's eyes. Then a weight crashed down over her, and all of it was gone.

KAT'S HEAD clunked down onto wet tile. Heavy. Dragging. Something squeaked and the pattering over her body stopped, a chill rolling up and over her. The rustle of fabric hitting the floor, then the crack and pop of muscles and bone shifting.

A tongue rasped over her face.

—Kat?—

Mmm. Her eyelids scrunched, a horrible pounding in her skull. Where was Kit? She groped at her consciousness, looking for her other half...

—Kat?— Darke's voice was full of worry, his tongue rougher. A paw pressed to her side.

Kat whimpered, her skin sister wasn't there, but how was that possible?

—KAT?— A nose snuffed at her, and she cracked an eye, blinking to focus.

—I'm here, Boy Vengeance... but I can't find Kit...—

—look deeper— His brows drew together, his markings blurring as the room spun. Darke's tongue rasped over her face again. He nuzzled at her ear. *—you're beautiful—*

Deeper? Kat chuffed her pleasure, slowly lifting her head.

—You're not so bad yourself.— She clambered to her feet, wobbling, then fell back onto her haunches. Damn. This was harder than it looked. Darke sat back, watching her with his tail wrapped around his paws, tip flicking.

—takes time—

We don't have time, she grumbled, water dripping off her fur. Gun shots and yelling came from the garage, and she hissed, claws scrabbling on the tile for purchase.

Darke didn't move. *—all the time, for you—*

Mmm. Kat dipped her head to groom herself, surprised and pleased her mate was such a charmer. She sneezed, spraying out a mouthful of water.

—shake first— He splayed his legs and demonstrated, bits of fur puffing out under the bathroom's fluorescents.

Kat watched him, her head cocked. She pushed up to stand. *—If I fall on my ass and you laugh, Imma be pissed.—*

Darke chuffed his amusement and turned his back. *—won't watch—*

She shot him a look to make sure he wasn't peeking and mimicked what he'd done. Water flung out from her coat, spraying over the bathroom. She sighed, feeling about thirty pounds lighter, and lifted a paw, licking between her toes.

—okay?—

—Mmm—

He turned, stalking around her in a tight circle. The hair on her nape tingled in anticipation. *—mine—* His brow rubbed against her cheek, his pheromones thick in her nostrils. *—claiming you soon, beautiful…—* His head cocked, pupils wavering. *—first, Kit?—*

Kat chuffed her annoyance, looking inward… traveling deep… her heart quailed. Damn. Her skin sister's consciousness was in a bad way. It curled around itself, a tight ball shoved into the recesses of their psyche, trembling.

—She's…not okay… I think she needs time.—

—time?—

—Yeah, time.—

Darke's form blurred, Leaving Grim crouched on the tiles before her. He extended a finger, tracing around one of her eyes, his face so fucking sad. "Then that's what we'll give her. I'll be out there when you're ready."

He pulled on his clothes and pushed through the door. Yelling and the sounds of things crashing filtering past.

Kat watched it swing back and forth before coming to a stop, her tail twitching. Her eyes narrowed, and she turned her attention back inward, pissed as fuck. Man would sacrifice himself and the entire crew waiting on Kit's ass.

Not. Fucking. Happening.

—Kit! You stupid, selfish bitch!—

The quavering ball of her skin-sister's consciousness went still.

—That's right, you need to get over your damned self and listen. There are people out there trying to save your dumb ass, and you're in here all poor fucking me. While you're wallowing, Reaper's on his damned way!—

Kit's thoughts unraveled, lashing out at her, and Kat jumped back.

Yeah, she'd thought that would get her attention.

Poor fucking me? I'm the selfish bitch? Excuse fucking me for taking a hot minute to wish shit wasn't so fucked up. I didn't ask for any of this, and I'm doing the best I fucking can!

Kat chuffed, grooming between her toes. *—I know, and it's embarrassing—*

Embar—fuck you!

—No, fuck you. First you throw a fucking hissy fit about me saving our asses on that mountain, then you almost kill us mid-shift, and now, oh, boo fucking hoo, the big bad lady lion won't let me shift back, we're feral. Cry me a fucking river. You want this form, fucking take it.—

I hate you.

—*You see me caring?*— Kat lifted a leg to lick her ass, and Kit's consciousness lunged at her, pushing her down.

CHAPTER TWELVE

GRIM PUSHED through the bathroom door, into pande-fucking-monium. Stitch was up in Deuce's face, with Doc beside him, glaring. Man wasn't wearing a shirt and looked guilty as fuck. Brick was on his ass laughing like a goddamned mental patient, a fucking hole blown through his shoulder, and Mouse was wrestling with Wrench, trying to hold him down so Triss could sedate him.

He kicked out blindly, and she fell back into a tool cart, flashing way too much of her bare ass beneath an oversized T. Shit, that's where Deuce's shirt had gone. As to where her panties had ended up… Grim groaned. No wonder Stitch was losing it… Christ, they didn't have time for this shit…

"The fuck?!" Grim yelled, his voice ringing with an alpha command.

Everyone in the room froze for half a heartbeat, then Triss sprang forward, jabbing Wrench with her hypodermic. He went limp, and Mouse climbed off him, groaning.

"Was his fault," the tech nerd sniffled, wiping a sleeve across his face. "Fucker took one look at Brick and pulled his piece. You owe me fifty bucks!" he called to Deuce.

"Yeah," Triss said, going over to triage Brick. Beneath the ragged, blood-stained hole in his shirt, he'd had already scabbed up. Triss sat back on her heels, eyeing the enforcer as he kept on cackling. She smacked him. "Asshole. You're lucky we're healing so fast now. That would've killed you."

"Fucker…" Wrench slurred, trying to roll up to sit.

"Worth it." Brick wiped his eyes. "Ah hah ha… did you see his face when I didn't go down?"

Triss stood, rolling her eyes, and turned to Grim. "Is Kit…?"

"She needs time," Grim swallowed, hating himself for pushing Kit to change before she was ready. He'd almost lost her in there and now… He knew exactly how deep inside her cat she was, how she felt… Christ, he'd been there for years after Reaper had banded him with silver.

And now he was no fucking better.

"Way I hear tell, we ain't got much time t'go around," Stitch growled. He and Doc were filthy as fuck, and the sergeant at arms was gripping the butt of his gun, still glaring at Deuce.

"Um, Mouse, why don't you help me get Wrench into the break room?" Triss asked, scowling at Brick when he stood. "Not you."

"Psh." The enforcer got up and leaned against the busted doorway. "Like I'd miss this."

"There is no 'this,' " Grim growled. "Triss and Kit were in the bathroom cleaning up. She got stuck shifting, and Triss ran out, half-dressed. Deuce gave her his shirt to cover up. End of story, right?"

Deuce's Adam's apple bobbed before he nodded, not meeting anyone's eye. Shit. What the fuck had happened?

Stitch's eyes narrowed. "Didn't fucking smell like nothin' with what the two of 'em were putting out. Motherfucker's too Goddamned old to be—"

"It's twelve years," Doc snapped. "You've done worse, fucking mollys half your age."

"Triss ain't a molly. She's my Goddamned daughter!" he roared.

"And Nikki's MK's," she spat back, "but that didn't stop you from sticking' your dick—"

"Jesus Fucking Christ, woman! This ain't about—" He took a deep breath, visibly calming himself as Deuce slunk away into the break room, Brick on his heels.

"You're right, 'cause there is no *us*." Doc shook her head, arms crossed and muttering to herself.

Grim ran a hand over his jaw at their perpetual argument on repeat. Best to just ignore it. "So… how was the trip up?"

Stitch snorted and pulled out his vape. "Lovely. We ran into MK tryin' to avoid that clusterfuck at the edge of town. Shit's hit the fan. That fucking vote went through last night. Mayhem's now affiliated with SV. They gave Shiv temporary presidency until the fucking table's repopulated with their people. Assholes is turning their back on everyone that went down to that moot. Says the club's official stance is we went rogue and since we're such old fuckin' friends, MK advised us to disappear. Asshole's real torn up about it. Gave us forty-five minutes before they're coming at us to clean house."

Grim's teeth grit together so hard they popped. "Nikki?"

"Hanna says that slut's moved into Clay's old room with Shiv and that other brother of yours," Doc spat. "Miser turned in his cut and went nomad. He ain't the only one, but God only knows if Reaper will let 'em get very far."

Grim nodded, pursing his lips and doubting that they would.

"We need some place to hole up, and this ain't it," Stitch muttered, toking on his vape with shaking hands.

"No, it's not…" Grim looked at Doc and tossed her his burner. "Call your sister."

She blanched. "Are you out of your fucking—"

"Yeah, probably," Grim snarled, spinning at her. "But seems to me if someone needs to disappear, Mama Roe's the one they go to. All we need is a hole to crawl into, otherwise, the rest of her family's gonna be buried in one six feet fucking deep next to Selena. Now make the fucking call!"

Doc took half a step back, then nodded, her jaw set.

Stitch clapped him on the shoulder. " 'Bout fuckin' time I heard that timbre in your voice… I told you, son. You're just as much an alpha as Clay was. Good t'see you finally owning it, even if that was a shit decision."

"Rest of the crew here?" Grim sighed, scrubbing at his hair.

"Nah," he said, shaking his grizzled head. "Rest of 'em peeled out t'go check on their families and get 'em somewhere safe. Steel and Decker hightailed it, goin' nomad, probably Royce, too. Don't imagine we'll be hearing from any of them anytime soon."

They both looked up as Doc came over, looking like she'd just been put through the wringer. "Says she's got a place that's stocked and defensible, but she's got conditions. She wants to meet."

"Where?"

"Cemetery off 4, half an hour."

Fuck. They both looked at him for approval and Grim's chest got tight.

"Yeah, pack up what we can here, and let's do it," he said, heading for the break room. Asorav was still on the phone in the far corner of the shop, his hand pinched across his temples. How he'd maintained a conversation with the rest of the shit going down… Whatever. Was probably more shit Grim didn't want to fucking hear.

Wrench was sitting at the break room table, lining up prescription bottles one way and then doing it over again another.

"Dude, just pick one, alphabetical or by height," Deuce said from beside him, his face buried in the nest of his arms.

"You say that like it's easy," the mechanic slurred.

"Yeah, Deucey, you're not taking the font size into

account," Brick said, eating more pilfered snacks. Triss sat across from him with way too many gum wrappers in front of her.

Wrench's eyes widened, his hand hovering over one of the bottles.

"I think you broke him," she said, snapping her gum.

Mouse glanced up at Grim. "Hey, man, everything good?"

"Fuck no. You guys up to speed?" Grunts chorused back at him. "Doc's sister's got a place to hole up, but she wants to meet at the cemetery off 4 first. No idea how this place is stocked, but it's supposed to be defensible. Pack whatever shit around here you think we can use. We're leaving in ten."

"Ten?" Wrench raised his head like it weighed about fifty pounds. Shit, how much of that stuff did Triss hit him with?

She turned like she'd heard him. "I might have given him a little bit too much," she said, not quite pinching her fingers together. "But trust me, it's better this way."

Wrench gave her a thumbs up, and what Grim was pretty sure was supposed to be a wink.

Yeah, no.

She eyed her med kit. "I might dose myself if we're meeting Auntie Roe. You know that's super stupid, right? She hates you."

"I'm aware," he muttered. "But we're still doing it."

The rest of the crew exchanged glances, then stood, going to make themselves useful. Grim flopped down into a chair by Mouse. "Anything else on there I need to know about?"

The tech nerd shrugged, sniffling. "I got that contact info you wanted, and I'm running a different algorithm on the data I pulled around the Cantone clusterfuck. No leads on who put out the contract on you... but about an hour ago, an encrypted file hit one of the dummy email servers I have set up. If I had my other rig, it'd be opened by now, but..."

"How long?"

"Longer than we got here. I'll do what I can, but until we set up shop somewhere, I'm gonna be dead in the water."

Grim nodded, frowning. "We'll figure it out."

Along with every fucking thing else.

KIT SAT SHIVERING on the bathroom floor. She wiped a hand across her eyes, pissed as hell. At her cat, at Grim… at her frickin' self. God. Kat was right, and Kit hated her for it. None of them had asked for any of this, and the man responsible, her fucking father, was just going on his merry way, wreaking havoc.

She needed to get her shit together.

Deep breath, Kit.

—That's my girl.—

She pulled herself up to glare into the mirror. *I swear to Christ, you ever try to lick your own ass again…*

—Then I guess we'll have to find someone to do it for us…—

Kit's cheeks pinked, glancing at the bags Triss had brought in. She pulled over the Hermès, pushing aside Brick's weird pouch with the vamp's phone. Even without Grim's jacket, it was still packed with—her fingers closed around cashmere. What the…?

A sob caught in her throat. Grim'd taken the sweater she'd been eyeing in the vamp's trophy closet, the jeans… oh God, that green dress and the Choos…

—Mmm, he's a keeper.—

Kit laughed, pulling them on. The cream sweater was streaked on one sleeve with shit from his cut, but sweet baby Jesus, how it felt against her skin… She shoved her feet into her boots, almost feeling like all was right with the world.

Kit sighed, running a hand through her hair and snagging her dirties. She hitched the bag over her shoulder and pushed out into the shop.

Stitch and Doc stood off to the side, arguing. Triss and the guys were packing things into the town car and the sports car in one of the bays that had a long scrape down its side. She saw Kit and ran over to hug her.

"Oh my God, I'm so glad you're not dead!"

Kit hugged her back. "Yeah, me too."

Triss held Kit by the shoulders, eyeing her outfit. "Damn. Now I feel all ugly step sister. This definitely calls for my pizza cat dress." She grinned, skipping off through the bathroom door.

Kit rolled her eyes, not even wanting to know what the hell that looked like, and caught sight of Mr. Asorav talking on the phone in the corner.

—No, he's not... he's talking with someone mind to mind again, like he did back at his apartment.—

Kit threw her bag into the town car's trunk. *Can you make it out this time?*

Kat was silent, then, *—Uh oh...—*

*What do you mean—*a hand wrapped around her biceps.

"A moment, Katherine, if you please?"

She smiled up at the vamp, trying not to look guilty as fuck. "Um... sure?"

"I understand the temptation to eavesdrop on one's elders, but strongly suggest you resist the urge," he said, looping her arm through his. "There are those that do not take kindly to such invasions of privacy."

Did you hear anything?

—No!—

"Which is why you're only getting a warning," the vamp said, patting her hand.

Kit swallowed the lump in her throat. "Vampires really can read minds? I thought—"

"Yes and no. Your compatriots' minds are closed to me, but it seems you and I share an affinity." He took in her expression and chuckled. "Yes, it surprised me as well. However, after Cecelia—"

"I want to know what you meant when you said she was elsewhere."

Mr. Asorav sighed. "I don't totally understand it, but I believe she's trapped somewhere between." His lips pursed at Kit's blank look. "It's… the place one goes to get from here to there. I'm afraid I can't explain it any better than that. She wasn't strong enough to anchor my form at this end, and when I pulled, she was sucked in."

"Because she was your heart. Aryanna told me you were a day-walker…"

"Did she now?" The vamp's brow quirked. "Intriguing that's she's so free with my personal concerns… unless she had some inkling of what was to come."

"Actually, it was Hillary who mentioned you couldn't be, um, de-animated, without your heart." Kit said, not liking the chill emanating from the vamp. "Don't worry, she's not around anymore to note it in the queen's memoir."

Mr. Asorav laughed. "How delightful. I never could understand how Aryanna abided that vitriolic shrew. I'm only sorry I wasn't there to see it, but suppose that's neither here nor there, and you, my dear, most certainly are… She told you, then, of my Maker's triumph?"

If that was what he wanted to call the witch's spell, she wasn't gonna argue. Kit nodded.

"Mmm." He pondered for a moment. "It's a metaphor, you know. She wasn't my heart, she *had* my heart. The spell transformed the physical organ and created a bridge, tying our life forces to those we held dearest. It was genius, really. Love is such a fickle thing, and given a vampire's life span, in most cases transfers quite organically before the object of our affection dies… or is lost, in this case."

He pulled the little dog's collar from his pocket, and Kit couldn't help but notice how much it looked like a woman's bracelet now that it wasn't around the little Pom's neck. Mr. Asorav turned her palm up, dropping it in, and closing her fingers around it. "And it seems once again, my heart has been captured by another. I assure you, I am aware this is most inconvenient, but, as I said, the heart wants what the heart wants, now, doesn't it?"

The way Kit's was pounding against her rib cage, hers wanted the fuck out.

"Mr. Asorav, what are you telling me?"

"That it has gone to you, my dear girl." He swept his thumb over her clenched knuckles. "Which gives me a vested interest in your safety and effectively makes my temporary plans permanent. Aryanna will be livid, especially given the fact that her release is conditional upon my return to the Spire, but as to why she willfully put herself in that position…"

Fuck Aryanna, Kit was working on her own case of indignation. "So what, you're gonna end up vaporizing me like your dog?"

"Heavens, no," he chuckled.

Actually fucking chuckled. Kit stepped back, about to go off on the motherfucker.

—*You go Kit, hit him!*—

The corners of his eyes crinkled as he smiled. "Quite frankly, I'm more worried about *you* vaporizing me."

Kit stepped back again. What?

"You figure out what your queen's deal is?" Grim asked, coming over with his hands jammed into his pockets. Kit turned from Mr. Asorav and pushed up under Grim's arm. He frowned at the bracelet, then let out a deep sigh and pulled her close.

—*Darke says your boy blames himself for that mess in the bathroom.*—

What? Why would he—

—*Psh. Girl, men think everything revolves around them. Case in point, Mr. "You have my fucking heart and there's not a damned thing you can do about it."*—

Mr. Asorav raised his brow and cleared his throat. Damn. Him listening in was gonna take some getting used to... *You think he can turn that off?*

"Yes." He smirked at Kit, answering both her and Grim, handing him the phone. "My contact reports that Aryanna has essentially put herself completely within Sama's power for reasons only she herself can fathom. My sect has been effectively sidelined, and I'm afraid I'm not willing to sit on the bench or fulfill the conditions of her release. I've had quite enough of the Spire. I was just telling Katherine that my plans to stay have become permanent for the foreseeable future."

Grim grunted, scratching his stubble.

"Mr. Asorav, when you were there... did you see the witch that helped Grim?" Kit asked, trying not to think of Chanté... which meant now she couldn't stop thinking about Chanté. Her eyes teared up, and Mr. Asorav frowned.

"No, but I wasn't in a particularly pleasant section, either. I'd imagine one of Sama's brood would be afforded somewhat preferential treatment... However—and I can't be one hundred percent certain about this—but I do believe I saw your mother when they were taking me in."

Kit's heart skipped a beat. "You did?"

The vamp nodded. "They wheeled an older woman on a gurney past me at one point, and I distinctly remember doing a double take. Her resemblance to you was quite striking, even with the age difference."

"MK made a comment that you look just like her," Grim said. "And one of Reaper's crew saw you dancing at Skin and thought the same thing."

"Yeah, growing up, my aunt used to tell me I could be her twin. Damn, I guess I screwed up Claymore's narrative about me being dead," she murmured, tucking her hair behind her ear. God, she so was stupid for taking that job. He'd tried to tell her… "He really was trying to protect me, wasn't he?"

"As I've said before, Claymore James was a brilliant strategist. Whatever he did, there was always a reason behind it, and more often than not, it was for the higher good."

Grim grunted, shoving his hands back into his pockets like something about that bothered him. "Right. We're about ready to head out. Think there's room in the town car, but I was gonna take my bike…"

"Your bike? How—? Can I ride with you?" Kit asked.

Grim bit his lip, looking her up and down, and smiled. "Yeah. If you're up for it."

"With you? I'm up for anything."

His grin widened to his ears as he led her to his ride. Brick and Stitch were already on two others, and the rest of the crew and Mr. Asorav had piled into the cars.

"I guess the crew got the Bobber out before the bomb went off and were going to send someone back for Stitch's. Him and Doc rode mine and Brick's up from the drop point." Grim handed her a helmet and his jacket. "We gotta get you one of these, along with a property cut."

"What about you? How will everyone know you're mine?"

"I was thinking about getting your name tattooed right about here." His finger sliced across his throat as he straddled his motorcycle.

—*Dayum, that's gonna be hot.*—

Kit licked her lips, agreeing, and very aware that she wasn't wearing any panties as she climbed on behind him. He stomped down, and the motorcycle roared to life. The crew waited for his nod, then took off out of the garage, and into the unknown.

NEXT IN THE SERIES

Kit -Kat

GRIM STALKED out of the break room, rifling his hair. How the fuck had everything gone to shit so fast? He blew the messy locks from his face and frowned, glancing around the garage—

And did a double take at the trio of bikes by the bay door. Brick and Wrench's hogs, and Grim's Bobber. How the fuck had that made it out of the city? Holy—He stumbled over to them, not quite believing it was real. One of the crew must've ridden it out of the garage before the club blew, which meant Stitch had left his down there…

Christ, he'd abandoned his bike to snag the Bobber? A lump gummed up Grim's throat. You only did that kind of shit for your alpha.

He swallowed, gritting his teeth and hating himself. How much of this shit could he have avoided if he'd just sucked it the fuck up and owned the position after Clay's murder?

Guess he'd never know.

Grim blinked, his eyes hot. Fingers trailing down the leather seat. Listening to the click and ping of the engine cooling. Avoiding the rest of the crew packing up. He frowned, guilt eating at him, his stomach a fucking mess. Staring at the bathroom door, willing it to open.

For Kit to come out on two legs.

Come on, baby… Hands down, she was his priority, but Jesus fuck, the rest of the crew depended on him, too, and they all needed to get gone. Clay's refusal to take a mate abruptly made more sense than Grim wanted it to. Some part of that equation was gonna get fucked, and he'd be damned if it was gonna be Kit unless she was squarely on his dick.

Kat say anything else to you? he asked his cat.

— no. fighting with Kit —

Grim grunted, the angst of having to choose between his mate and his club landing a gut punch of shame. Christ, he knew what that was like. Being at odds with your beast. The terror of feeling trapped inside yourself, of sinking down so fucking deep you didn't know if you could come back...

[CHAGRIN]

— different —

Same, Grim snapped. Shit was close enough, less the cuffs. He rubbed at the scars on his wrists, the lines of ink blurred and broken. The memory of the snick of silver setting his teeth on edge. That creeping, seeping burn infecting his veins with its poison...

He wiped the sweat from his brow. Yeah, he knew how it felt, and granted, he wasn't keeping her there, but he'd fucking sent Kit on that spiral inward by pushing her to change. Jesus, he was a piece of shit. A sad laugh slid from his lips.

But fuck, that's what everyone thought anyway, wasn't it? The media, the rest of Mayhem... Mama Roe sure as hell did, and he was about to go kiss her fucking—

Grim's breath caught as the bathroom door swung open and Kit strode out, looking classy as fuck and like the last person he should be with. Triss dropped the crap she was packing into the cage's trunk and ran over to hug her.

Christ, he wanted to do the same... but, damn. Grim wet his lips. Kit wasn't... Damn. She was wearing that soft sweater he'd snagged from the vamp queen's trophy closet. Shit was fucking sinful the way it hung off her shoulders, then clung to her tits. The jeans she'd been so crazy about did the same to her hips, a sliver of her flat stomach flashing as she raised her arms to hug the girl back. And when Triss skipped away and Kit turned toward the cages?

Woman was a fucking goddess.

Grim bit back a groan at the way her long black hair dusted her ass as she bent to put her bag in the trunk. She looked like a million fucking bucks, which was easily nine hundred ninety-nine thousand and change above his pay grade.

— ours —

The pang in Grim's chest echoed the truth of that statement. Maybe he didn't deserve her now, but he'd fucking bust his ass until he did. *If she still wants us.* His throat bobbed at the possibility she wouldn't after what he'd done to her.

— asked to shift —

Yeah, but the idea of being a shifter versus the reality of it were two very different things, and Grim'd only known Kit for a hot fucking minute. When they'd met, she'd been so damned adamant she didn't want to change...

— Reaper decided for her —

Grim's knuckles whitened. *And he's gonna die for it.* Darke chuffed in agree—

A growl welled up in Grim's throat, his eyes narrowing.

Asorav had ended his call and wrapped his hand around Kit's arm, pulling her off to the side. He spoke to her adamantly in hushed tones in the next bay.

— listen? —

Yeah. Grim stepped back into the shadows, his hearing sharpening.

Kit was smiling up at the vamp like he'd caught her at something. She was trying to play it off as he was talking. "... understand the temptation to eavesdrop on one's elders, but strongly suggest you resist the urge." Asorav looped her arm through his, and a muscle in Grim's jaw twitched at the asshole's familiarity with her.

— known her longer —

Don't remind me, Grim muttered. He still couldn't believe Kit had been the Darkling's dog walker.

"There are those that do not take kindly to such invasions of privacy," the vamp scolded.

Kit's eyes widened, her pupils waffling—

Grim did a double take. *Shit, did I really see that?* Aside from the mirror, he'd never seen anyone else's flip between theirs and their beast's.

— did. Kat's scared. won't talk —

He bit back a growl. Was that fucking right?

"Which is why you're only getting a warning." The vamp patted her hand like some kind of benevolent fucking uncle. Grim's lip curled, knowing that grift all too well. He was gonna beat the shit outta—

"Vampires really can read minds?" Kit squeaked. "I thought—"

Wait, what? He froze.

"Yes and no," Asorav said. "Your compatriots' thoughts are closed to me, but it seems you and I share an affinity." The asshole chuckled. "Yes, it surprised me as well. However, after Cecelia—"

"I want to know what you meant when you said she was elsewhere."

Asorav sighed, and Grim had to smirk at Kit's indignation over the MIA Pomeranian. "I don't totally understand it," the vamp said, "but I believe she's trapped somewhere between. It's... the place one goes to get from here to there. I'm afraid I can't explain it any better than that. She wasn't strong enough to anchor my form at this end, and when I pulled, she was sucked in."

Well, that sounded like total bullshit, but Grim supposed the prick couldn't admit to killing the thing. In either case, Kit sounded like she bought it.

"Because she was your heart. Aryanna told me you were a day-walker."

"Did she now…"

Grim scratched his stubble, wondering how much of an issue that was gonna be. Vampires were enough of a pain in the ass at night. One lurking around 24/7 didn't exactly give him the warm fuzzies, but then again, this conversation didn't either.

"…mentioned you couldn't be, um, de-animated, without your heart." Kit said, rubbing her arms like she was cold. "Don't worry, she's not around anymore to note it in the queen's memoir."

Asorav laughed, and Grim wanted to smash his fist through the vamp's fangs. "How delightful. I never could understand how Aryanna abided that vitriolic shrew. I'm only sorry I wasn't there to see it, but suppose that's neither here nor there, and you, my dear, most certainly are… She told you, then, of my Maker's triumph?"

Kit nodded like she was humoring him. Grim rolled his eyes. Fucking vamps had sticks shoved up their asses almost as far as the witches. Christ, they were pretentious fucks.

"It's a metaphor, you know," Asorav said. "She wasn't my heart, she *had* my heart. The spell transformed the physical organ and created a bridge, tying our life forces to those we held dearest. It was genius, really. Love is such a fickle thing, and given a vampire's life span, in most cases transfers quite organically before the object of our affection dies… or is lost, in this case."

He pulled a wide, platinum bracelet from his pocket, studded with what Grim was positive were diamonds, and closed Kit's fingers around it. The fuck? "And it seems once again, my heart has been captured by another. I assure you, I am aware this is most inconvenient, but, as I said, the heart wants what the heart wants, now, doesn't it?"

Grim bared his teeth, knuckles white as he clenched his fists. Did that motherfucker just give Kit a fucking king's ransom in jewelry and tell her he loved her?

—no, his heart—

I don't give a fuck, she's MINE.

— no, stupid listen —

His cat's censure snapped Grim out of his rage. *Listen? Since when do you—*

"Mr. Asorav, what are you telling me?"

"That it has gone to you, my dear girl." The vamp swept his thumb over her knuckles. "Which gives me a vested interest in your safety and effectively makes my temporary plans permanent. Aryanna will be livid, especially given that her release is conditioned upon my return to the Spire, but as to why she willfully put herself in that position…"

— see? she dies, he dies —

Holy fuck. The furry prick was right. That's why Asorav was playing third wheel. If Reaper or the witches got hold of Kit, the vamp was fucked…

"So what, you're gonna end up vaporizing me like your dog?" Grim's attention snapped back to Kit at the fury in her voice. A smile slid across his face. *That's my girl…*

— ours —

"Heavens, no," the condescending prick chuckled.

Kit stepped back like she was gonna deck him, and Grim adjusted himself. Goddamn, she was fucking fierce, but she needed to save it util they were some place safe. Time to end this.

The vamp smiled like he thought it was cute. "Quite frankly, I'm more worried about *you* vaporizing *me.*"

And if Kit didn't, Grim fucking would.

"You figure out what your queen's deal is?" he asked, walking over with his hands jammed into his pockets to hide his semi. Kit turned from Mr. Asorav and pushed up under Grim's arm where she belonged. He let out a deep sigh at the rightness of it, pulling her close.

Asorav raised his brow and cleared his throat like he had a problem with it. Grim made a note to do it more.

"Yes." The vamp smirked at Kit, and handed Grim the phone. "My contact reports that Aryanna has essentially put herself completely within Sama's power for reasons only she herself can fathom. My sect has effectively been sidelined, and I'm afraid I'm not willing to sit on the bench or fulfill the conditions of her release. I've had quite enough of the Spire. I was just telling Katherine that my plans to stay have become permanent for the foreseeable future."

No, he wasn't willing to let Kit run around unattended, but that sounded plausible. Vamp was slicker than fucking snot. Grim grunted, scratching his stubble.

"Mr. Asorav, when you were there… did you see the witch that helped Grim?" Kit asked.

He hugged her closer. Kit's bestie being locked up in the Spire was fucking killing her. Grim didn't know how to make that better, but he owed Chanté a debt. One way or another, he'd pay it. He kissed the top of Kit's head and Asorav frowned.

"No, but I wasn't in a particularly pleasant section, either. I'd imagine one of Sama's brood would be afforded somewhat preferential treatment… However—and I can't be one hundred percent certain about this—but I do believe I saw your mother when they were taking me in."

"You did?" Kit went still and Grim bit back a swear. Vamp was a fucking asshole for waving that carrot in front of her right now.

Asorav nodded. "They wheeled an older woman on a gurney past me at one point, and I distinctly remember doing a double take. Her resemblance to you was quite striking, even with the age difference."

"MK made a comment that you look just like her," Grim said, totally getting why Reaper and Clay had both wanted to bang the woman, but the shitstorm that'd followed? Grim still didn't understand that. Regardless, the resemblance was how

SV had found Kit. "And one of Reaper's crew saw you dancing at Skin and thought the same thing."

"Yeah, growing up, my aunt used to tell me I could be her twin. Damn, I guess I screwed up Claymore's narrative about me being dead," Kit murmured, tucking her hair behind her ear. "He really was trying to protect me, wasn't he?"

"As I've said before, Claymore James was a brilliant strategist. Whatever he did, there was always a reason behind it, and more often than not, it was for the higher good."

Grim grunted at the knife to the spine those words delivered, the blackness of the first eighteen years of his life burbling up from the abyss.

A reason for it. A purpose behind all the shit Reaper had done to him. Made him do.

Too bad Grim didn't have a clue what the fuck that reason was.

— bad times —

Yeah. He shoved his hands back into his pockets. "Right. We're about ready to head out. Think there's room in the town car, but I was gonna take my bike…"

"Your bike? How—? Can I ride with you?" Kit asked.

Grim bit his lip and smiled, so fucking glad she'd taken the bait. "Yeah. If you're up for it."

"With you? I'm up for anything."

His grin widened, eager to test that statement out.

BOOKS BY AK NEVERMORE

THE DAE DIARIES - URBAN FANTASY WITH SPICE

One Night in Bliss — FREE TO READ

Flame & Shadow

Air & Darkness — (August 2024)

Playing with Fire — (October 2024)

THE PRICE OF TALENT - STEAMY DARK SCI-FI ROMANTASY

Breeder — FREE TO READ

Breaker

Destroyer — FREE TO READ

Binder — (September 2024)

Split — (November 2024)

Overlord — (January 2024)

THE MAW OF MAYHEM - PARANORMAL MC EROTICA

Bites of Mayhem — FREE TO READ

The Maw of Mayhem — FREE TO READ

Grimdarke

Darker

Kit-Kat — (May 2024)

Katherine — (July 2024)

ABOUT THE AUTHOR

AK Nevermore writes science fiction and urban fantasy. She enjoys operating heavy machinery, freebases coffee, and gives up sarcasm for Lent every year.

A Jane-of-all-trades, she's a certified chef, restores antiques, and dabbles in beekeeping when she's not reading voraciously or running down the dream in her beat-up camo Chucks.

Unable to ignore the voices in her head, and unwilling to become medicated, she writes full time. Her books explore dark worlds, perversely irreverent and profound, and always entertaining.

Want more Nevermore?
Sign up for her newsletter and never miss a release!

9 798988 746430